It was blood. . . .

So you took a few tumbles. Someone would pick up the pieces. Having a good time was what counted, as long as no one got hurt.

Hurt.

Why did her shoes hurt so much?

She looked down at her feet. They were so far away.

It wasn't her red shoes at all. Her red shoes wouldn't leave smeared red footprints. Make long red smears on her sheets. It wasn't her red shoes.

It was blood.

Other Point paperbacks
you will enjoy:

The Snowman by R.L. Stine

Teacher's Pet by Richard Tankersley Cusick

Slumber Party by Christopher Pike

Final Exam by A. Bates

Prom Dress by Lael Littke

point

SISTER DEAREST

D. E. ATHKINS

SCHOLASTIC INC.
New York Toronto London Auckland Sydney

ISBN 0-590-44941-9

12 11 10 9 8 7 6 5 4 3 2 1   1 2 3 4 5 6/9

Printed in the U.S.A.   01

First Scholastic printing, November 1991

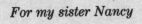

For my sister Nancy

Chapter 1

Vicki Clements stopped to stare up at the big old brick building. Good old Amelia Earhart High! She was glad to be back, back to normal. Then she smiled ruefully and shook her head. Whoever thought she'd call it normal, being happy to be back at school?

"You'll be okay, babe?" Alaina Clements gave her younger sister's elbow a reassuring squeeze. Beside them, their brother Alan Clements suddenly snorted, and slouched off.

Alaina looked after her twin, frowning, then switched her attention back to Vicki. "I'm fine," said Vicki quickly. "You go on."

"Are you sure?"

Unaccountably, Vicki felt irritated. "Of course I'm sure. What could be wrong?"

Alaina let go of Vicki's arm. "Well, if you're sure . . . I've got a Deltas meeting this afternoon . . ."

"I can find my own way home. You and your sorority siblings can party hearty, okay? No cares."

"Vicki. The Deltas are not — " Alaina stopped,

then smiled slightly. "Okay. Don't try to do too much now."

Before Vicki could answer, Alaina had drifted up the stairs in that peculiar, ethereal way she had, to be surrounded immediately by her classmates. Good old Alaina, thought Vicki. With her, a little guilt went a long, long way.

Suddenly a husky voice whispered in her ear, "Hey, it's Dorothy and her ruby slippers!"

"Hey!" Vicki turned and grinned.

"Hey, yourself," said Janet Peretti. She nodded toward the flashy red shoes Vicki was wearing. "Proud and loud, huh?"

"Absolutely. It may not go with jeans, but who cares?"

"Sexy. *Verrry* sexy, is what I say, and that goes with anything! Hey, they're not just shoes, they're art!"

"As the next Georgia O'Keeffe, you ought to know!" Vicki laughed and shifted her pack to the other arm. She really *was* glad to be back.

"I saw Her Highness leaving," Janet went on. "What'ja do, click the heels together three times and make her disappear?"

"Don't start on Alaina, Janet . . ."

Janet held up her hand. "Right. As an only child, what do I know? Listen . . ."

Skillfully heading off Vicki's protest, Janet launched into her typical patter of hot gossip and inconsequential details as they made their way up the stairs.

That was one thing about Janet. She always knew what was going on, and she probably wasn't kidding when she said she knew more dirt on more people than anyone outside the CIA *and* the FBI.

But, for whatever reason Janet didn't like Alaina, she kept it to herself. She knew just how far to go. And Vicki cut her a lot of slack. After all, she and Janet had known each other forever.

Realizing now that Janet was chattering to keep her from being nervous, Vicki felt a rush of affection for her friend. *She's closer than a sister*, she thought. *I'd trust her with my life.*

Then out of nowhere, Marty Harmon angled up to them with his peculiar, stiff-legged strut.

He doesn't look real, thought Vicki. He looks like a zombie.

He stopped and stared at Vicki with hot, intense eyes. "You're back."

"From the dead," said Vicki flippantly, trying for a light touch.

Only it didn't work. He smiled, slowly. "Maybe," he said. Then he cut back into the crowd and was gone.

"What a creep," said Janet.

Vicki took a deep breath. Once — before the accident — she'd thought his stiff, cocky walk, his stand-up hair, even his graveled skin, made him sexy. But then she'd looked into *his* soul and seen — nothing. Now, she assured herself, he doesn't mean anything to me. We've broken up. He's history. Just a sleazy version of Rod Stewart. Not, in Vicki's opinion, that there was any version of Rod Stewart that wasn't sleazy.

"Uh-oh," Janet muttered. "If Marty comes, can Caddie be far behind . . ."

Sure enough, like the pilot fish after the shark, Caddie Melville slipped out of the crowd from Marty's wake.

"You're back," she said, unconsciously parroting Marty's words.

"I have a big fat shadow that goes in and out with me," breathed Janet, so only Vicki could hear.

"Hello, Caddie," said Vicki as calmly as she could.

"Too bad," Caddie answered.

"Too bad I didn't die? Is that it Caddie?"

"You said it. I didn't," hissed Caddie. Then she was gone, too.

Blindly, without thinking, Vicki started forward.

"Slow down," said Janet. "She's nothing but frustrated pond scum. She wants Marty."

"She can have him," said Vicki.

"What did you ever see in him, anyway?"

Vicki sighed. "I don't know. I guess I thought underneath that shallow veneer there was a warm, sensitive, intelligent human being."

"Talk about great expectations!" Janet shook her head.

"Yeah, well I found out, didn't I? Underneath that veneer is — more veneer. A shallow darkness. Too bad he won't get together with Caddie. They were made for each other."

"Sure. Except neither of them knows the meaning of true love. I mean, look at the only people they've ever really fallen in love with."

"Themselves," guessed Vicki.

"Gold star for you."

Janet skipped ahead to a new subject. Her next

words made Vicki forget all about Marty and Caddie.

"Heard about the nun?"

"Nun?"

"I mean ex-nun. Can you believe it? This is where your tax dollars are going!"

"Whoa! Slow down! What *are* you talking about?"

"The new principal — Ms. Mary Sewell. They say she's a *failed nun*. And you know what that means."

"No, what does that mean?" Vicki teased.

"Well. Locked away! No outlets. *You know . . .*"

"Oh, Janet!" Shaking her head, Vicki allowed herself to be borne along on the tide of people and talk into her homeroom class.

Janet was still talking — this time about Alan — as they drifted out of homeroom and toward first-day assembly in the gym.

"Your brother is major gorgeous. Have I said that before, Vick?"

"He can be a major pain. And yes, you've said it before." Vicki waved at someone across the hall. It really was great being back. Amelia E. was such a cool place, low-key, fun. Everyone was being so terrific. And more than one person had shown a proper appreciation of her shoes — and had offered to help.

But she didn't need help, not now. She was tough enough to make it on her own . . . even if the shoes did pinch a little.

Intent on her own thoughts, lulled by Janet's

talk, Vicki didn't realize where she was going until she'd gotten there and smacked into a tall figure lounging near the entrance of the gym. Teetering on the high-heeled shoes, trying to keep a grip on her backpack, she grabbed for balance, and dragged the figure back against the wall with her. For one moment she felt his body pressed against hers. For one moment, she stared into incredible blue eyes. My god, she thought. Oh my god.

Then Dace Jordon was stepping back, sliding his hands down her arms to her elbows, helping her get her balance. "You okay?" he drawled.

"Fine," she breathed. "Terrific." She felt the color rush up her neck and face. Dace looked at her, smiling, a moment longer, then let his eyes drop slowly down. "Nice shoes," he said, and then he was gone, sliding through the crowd on the way into the gym.

"Tooo much," cried Janet. "Dace Jordon! The most gorgeous . . . except for Alan . . . tell me *everything*, Vicki. . . . Was it good for you?"

Vicki felt her face get even redder. "Janet!" she hissed and, shifting her backpack, swung toward the door — and was rocked back on her heels a second time. Only this time she saw the person before the collision — no tall, dark, handsome senior, but a squat figure in a navy linen suit and sensible flat shoes. "Oof," she said, thinking at the same time, I can't believe it, people really do say oof.

It was like running into a brick wall.

"Excuse me," she gasped. "I'm so sorry. I . . ."

"You should watch your step, young woman," a sandpaper voice said.

"I'm sorry. Really," said Vicki. She looked down from the lofty heights of her shoes into the strangely smooth, somehow ageless face of the woman glaring back at her. Light glinted off the thick lens of wire-rimmed glasses.

"Sorry," the woman rasped. "It's easy to say you're sorry. Isn't it — Vicki."

"W-what?"

"Watch your step," the woman repeated and, turning, whisked into the gym.

Staring after her, Vicki heard Janet's gurgle of horrified delight. "You've done it now, Vick. Good work. That was the new principal — Ms. Failed Nun herself!"

It was true. Sitting high up in the bleachers, Vicki watched and listened as the navy blue figure was introduced as "Mary Sewell, your new principal."

The new principal's words matched her outfit, Vicki thought. No garbage about new beginnings and a new year. She started right in, waling on them.

"My name is Mary Sewell. I don't believe that the princi*pal* is your *pal*."

A few people snickered, but quickly stopped as Mary Sewell swept the room with an icy glare. She went on. "You will, however, call me Principal Sewell. You will be addressed, by me, by your surnames. There are going to be some changes around here. I believe in order and discipline. You earn the privileges of adults by proving that you can behave like adults."

She stopped again and surveyed the room. Even though she was sitting high in the bleachers, too high for Principal Sewell to see her, Vicki felt that icy gaze right to her bones.

Great, she thought. Just when you thought it was safe to go back to the classroom.

Chapter 2

"It's for you." Alaina held the receiver out as Vicki came out of her room, headed for dinner. She lowered her voice. "It's a *guy*."

"Great." Vicki groaned. "It's probably Marty." She took the receiver.

"Hello."

"Is this the lady in the red shoes?"

"Oh." Dace! Vicki looked up. Alaina was still standing there, smiling. "Hold on a minute, please." Vicki put her hand over the phone. "I'll be right down."

Alaina nodded and kept smiling. And kept standing there.

Vicki lowered the receiver and spoke as if she were making something clear to a child. "I'll be right down to dinner. Cover for me with Dad, okay?"

This time her space cadet sister got it. She nodded again and gave Vicki a little wave of her fingers, for all the world as if she were on the homecoming stage. Then she glided along the hallway.

Just to be safe, Vicki waited until her sister had gone down the stairs — it seemed to take forever — then said, "I do have a pair of red shoes."

"Good. I have a notebook that belongs to a lady with a pair of red shoes. This is Dace."

"I know. I mean, it must have fallen out of my backpack when I, uh, ran into you today." Oh, god, she was so dumb. Why remind him of what a klutz she'd turned into!

"That's what I thought. So, why don't I bring it by your locker tomorrow. After school?"

"My locker." Get a grip on yourself, Vicki. "My locker. Sure. It's number 269. Down by the back door."

"I'll be there," he said, and hung up.

" 'Bye," she said.

"Next time Janet calls, tell her to do it after the dinner hour," Rutland Clements said as Vicki slid into her place at the table.

"Janet?"

"Getting a homework assignment, right?" prodded Alaina.

Vicki threw her sister a quick, grateful look, then said, "I'll remind her, Dad."

"Good," he said. "How was your first day of school? You didn't push yourself? You look tired."

"No!"

Rutland Clements examined his younger daughter's face suspiciously. "You're awfully flushed."

"Uh — I'm trying some new makeup." *Like how to make up to Dace Jordon.*

Ellen Clements said, unexpectedly, "You have to be careful dear. Too much of that stuff makes you look cheap."

Alan snorted.

"That's enough!" said Mr. Clements.

Alaina interrupted. "Dad. We have a new principal. Really odd."

"Oh? Oh, yes." Their father turned his intense gray eyes on his older daughter. "The school board went and got a disciplinarian. About time. There isn't anything I haven't seen practicing criminal law, and there isn't anything you young people wouldn't do!"

"Now, dear." Mrs. Clements smiled vaguely around the table.

"Daddy!" Alaina made her mouth into a mock pout.

Mr. Clements looked quickly at his wife, then said, "You know, when I was young . . ."

"Daddy, you're not old!" Alaina, always the peacemaker.

What a Pollyanna, thought Vicki disgustedly.

"Flattery will get you nowhere, young lady. As I was saying . . ."

Grateful that the conversation and the evening were in safe channels, at least until dessert, Vicki slipped into thoughts of what she'd wear tomorrow to meet Dace. Something tight. Painted on. With a long sweater so her father wouldn't see it and object. He was so much stricter with her than with Alaina and Alan. A real disciplinarian . . .

And her red shoes. Definitely her red shoes.

Her red shoes.

They were killers. But then she liked to take chances. What was life for if you didn't take chances? Alaina might be Daddy's little girl, but Vicki was Daddy's little daredevil. She could make people sit up and take notice, even if she wasn't beautiful.

Even if she wasn't perfect.

So you took a few tumbles. Someone would pick up the pieces. Having a good time was what counted, as long as no one got hurt.

Hurt.

Why did her shoes hurt so much?

She looked down at her feet. They were so far away.

It wasn't her red shoes at all. Her red shoes wouldn't leave smeared red footprints. Make long red smears on her sheets. It wasn't her red shoes.

It was blood.

She woke up trying to scream. Choking on screams that couldn't come out. She could hear the choking sounds in the silent room in the silent house. She couldn't stop. Maybe when she stopped choking, it would mean she'd stop breathing. . . .

Her feet!

Vicki lurched up and yanked the covers aside. Her long pale legs gleamed in the streetlight that came through the window. Faint spidery webs of old scars, like vampire incisions, gleamed here and there, grim reminders of the accident . . . but that was all. It was okay.

It was just a dream, she told herself. Just a dream. Relax. Go to sleep. Forget about it. It was just an accident. And it was just a dream.

Her father started in on her right away the next

morning. "You look pale," he barked.

"I'm fine." She wasn't. Her head hurt. And the nightmare stayed there, at the edge of her consciousness.

"You're not eating."

She picked up her fork and pushed the bits of bacon around on the plate. Ugh. Across from her, Alaina was carefully dividing an English muffin into sections, spreading each section with raspberry jam, then nibbling it delicately. Alan was slouched over coffee, staring at nothing. Their mother was eating her way methodically through a bowl of fruit and yogurt.

Double ugh, thought Vicki. The red of the raspberries was particularly repellent. She turned her head away as Alaina, catlike, licked a fleck of red from the corner of her mouth.

"Vicki!"

Vicki jumped. "Sir?"

"Eat your breakfast."

"I'm not hungry! Why should I have to eat my breakfast when no one else does?"

"That's beside the point."

"It doesn't hurt for Vicki to learn to watch what she eats," their mother volunteered.

"Ellen!"

Their mother remained unflustered. "Or you either, dear."

Their father began to sputter.

"Daddy . . ." began Alaina.

Just then Alan reached out — and knocked over the tomato juice. It cascaded across the spotless white tablecloth, ruining it.

"Look what you've done." The veins in Rutland Clements' head stood out. "What is wrong with you!"

Alan shrugged.

Vicki watched in fascination as the tomato juice spread. I will *not* be sick, she told herself.

Alan stood up. "Gotta be going," he said. "School calls."

Mr. Clements stood up, too. "What about this mess?"

Alan half-raised his sleepy eyelids, then shrugged again.

"What about it?" he said.

"It's that attitude, that's the reason you're having to repeat your last semester. What has gotten into you? I've just about had it. . . ."

Vicki slipped away quickly from the table to the bathroom.

I will not be sick, I will not be sick, I will not be sick.

She conjured up Dace's face, the way he'd felt against her. She began to feel a little better.

She had to get to school. She had to go to school today.

Dace was waiting for her.

"You're not eating?"

"I'm fine," snapped Vicki. The noise in the lunch-room was overwhelming. The smell of the food was worse.

"Hey, take it easy! It's me. Janet?"

"Sorry." Vicki made herself smile. "Nervous about this afternoon, I guess."

Leaning her ample chest against the edge of the table, Lolly Parsons said, "You just — ran into him — huh?"

"Yeah."

Lolly wriggled happily, like a friendly blonde spaniel. "You are sooo lucky. What are you going to say?"

"I don't know. Hello."

"How about, 'Hello, gorgeous, how was heaven when you left?' "

Janet broke in. "Vick?"

Vicki took a deep breath, then spoke brightly, trying to erase the concern on her friend's face. "It's okay, Jan, really. I just had a bad night. I'm just tired, is all."

"Those dreams again."

"Naughty dreams — about Dace!" Lolly made her eyes round. "Oh, Vicki, you are too much."

"Hey, Lolly," said Janet, "isn't that Tim over there?"

"It can't be. It's not his lunch period."

"I'm sure of it," said Janet.

Lolly stood up and stared.

"Just left, I think. Some babe was with him . . ."

"Thanks, Janet," said Lolly. "See ya."

"Uh-huh." Janet sat back. "You know, Vick, maybe it would help to talk to somebody."

"For. Get. It! I'm not crazy."

"I know you're not. But after all you went through — "

Vicki felt the rage building up inside her, a red flood of it, scorching her veins. "Forget it, I said!

I thought that was what friends were for — to listen. But obviously you're not!"

So angry she could hardly see, Vicki pushed away from the table and stumbled out of the lunchroom. She didn't know how she found her way to the back steps, but she did. She sat down and leaned back and took deep breaths, the way she had done to get through the pain.

Get a grip, she told herself. Or people really will think you're crazy.

It's just that I'm so sick of being treated like an invalid. It was just a dumb accident.

Suddenly she remembered a conversation, the fragment of a conversation between her mother and her father. They'd been sitting by her bed as she drifted in and out of a drugged and painridden sleep.

"Crazy kids." Her father. "Fooling around in that car that way. What could she have been thinking of, to stand up like that? And what was Alan thinking of, to let her!"

Her mother's voice. Thoughtful. "Rutland? Honey? What if it wasn't an accident?"

Silence. Then her father. "Nonsense. Next thing I know, you'll be saying all that garbage about kids being accident-prone to get attention is true!"

No. An accident. Nobody's fault. Not hers. They'd all been spinning, cruising, hanging out. Spring fever. Having a great time.

And then she'd stood up. Pretending to be the homecoming queen, riding on the back of the float.

Alan's silver '57 T-bird was perfect for that. They'd been holding on to her. It was safe. It just looked wild and crazy.

And then she'd been flying.

They said Alan had swerved.

She didn't remember. Just the flight. Something about it. Free. The truth shall make you free.

I'm Peter Pan, look at me, I'll live forever. She smiled benevolently down on the others, so far away, so wrapped up in their own world.

Look at me.

She didn't remember coming down. Didn't remember anything after Peter Pan.

Didn't remember anything until she woke up in the middle of summer, in a world of pain.

They'd been worried she wouldn't pull through.

But she had. She'd proven them all wrong. So she wasn't beautiful and perfect like her sister. She wasn't mysterious and hot like her brother. But she was strong.

She could do anything. Why couldn't they just remember that, and forget the rest?

I'm never good enough, she thought, no matter what I do. It's never enough.

"Clements, I believe?" There was no mistaking the sandpaper voice.

Vicki turned slowly toward it, blinking back the tears. Principal Sewell.

"Answer me," said the principal.

"Vicki Clements."

"Stand up," said the principal. "Do you have a pass to be here?"

"No. I . . . I felt sick." Vicki couldn't meet those strange green eyes. She looked down at her feet. Stand on your own two feet, she thought. She looked up again.

The principal's expressionless face hadn't changed. "I know about you, Clements. And no one is getting away with anything in my school. Because I'm watching. You." She stepped aside. "Next time go to the nurse's office. If I catch you without a pass again, or proper authorization, you'll be suspended."

"Suspended!"

"You may go."

Willing herself not to hurry, Vicki went. She looked back once. The squat, strange figure was standing outlined in the doorway staring.

Staring at her.

Chapter 3

He wasn't there.

She walked down the hall, trying to look carefree and unconcerned. Feeling how deliciously tight her jeans were. I know how I look, she thought. And I'm glad.

But as she got further down the hall, she realized it didn't matter.

She saw a shining golden head at her locker. For a moment she thought it was Alan. No. Alaina. Alaina who always stood out, who could make even the grungy gray lockers look good, lighting up the hall, smiling, waving, talking to people.

Vicki slowed down. Even if he had been there, he'd be talking to Alaina. He wouldn't even remember her name.

She came to a stop in front of Alaina, pulling her backpack protectively across her chest. "Hi," she said.

"*There* you are," said Alaina. "We had a meeting. I thought I'd come by and see if you wanted to walk home."

"You didn't have to do that." Mechanically, she

opened her locker, and begin to dump things in it.

"What else are sisters for?"

Vicki didn't answer.

"Vicki? Dace was here when I got here."

I bet he was.

"He asked me to give you this."

I bet he did.

"Not bad, little sister. Dace Jordon."

I hate her. I wish she were dead. I could kill her.

Vicki straightened up.

"I'm ready when you are," she said.

Alaina rested her fingertips lightly on Vicki's arm as they walked down the front steps. Typical Alaina — fey, elusive, never quite touching anyone, always just out of reach. Vicki had never really noticed it before. Now she did. And she hated it.

It's one thing for a cat to think it's too good to touch anyone, she thought.

"So, Dace! Not bad, little sister."

"I guess." *Did he ask you out, big sister?*

"A lot better than Marty Harmon."

"A lot."

"He thinks he is such a stud. Marty Hormone is more like it." Alaina laughed. Vicki didn't.

Alaina turned and studied Vicki's face. "Are you okay?"

"Fine."

"No, you're not? What's wrong?"

"Nothing!"

Alaina suddenly let go of Vicki's arm, lifted her hand to her face. "Are you sure? Ever since the accident . . ."

"The accident, the accident, I'm sick of the accident!" There it was again, that separate animal that lived inside of her, raging to get out, to rip the whole world into bloody shreds . . . to let her find out just how nice it would be to give Alaina a push, a little push down all those stairs in front of them, leading out of the school. A little fall right out the front door. An ungraceful exit.

Because even a cat doesn't always land on its feet. Instead she took a deep breath and smiled her sunniest smile at Alaina. Alaina, who had been looking wary — no, it couldn't be — smiled back. She gave a little purring chuckle as they started down the stairs to the parking lot.

"No Deltas meeting today?"

"Vicki, our meetings are always on Mondays. You know that."

"Right . . . so how is *your* sorority?"

Shaking her head slightly, but still smiling, Alaina answered seriously, as Vicki knew she would. "It's not my sorority. We're not even a sorority, really. We're a service organization."

"Right," said Vicki. "A very, very exclusive one. . . ."

A voice called them.

It was Marty.

"Vicki. Alaina."

Vicki kept walking, but Alaina stopped, letting go of Vicki's arm. After a few more steps, Vicki stopped, too.

Marty's shadow fell between them, and Alaina stepped aside. Marty didn't seem to notice Alaina.

"Ring around the rosie," he intoned. "You know

the rhyme? It's really about the plague. The black plague. It's a description of the disease. . . ."

"Please," murmured Alaina, her eyelashes fluttering.

Marty lowered his voice, his eyes dark and brooding. "The plague. Think about it: upstairs, downstairs, we all fall down. Everybody dies, no matter who you are. Everybody."

"Thank you for sharing that, Marty," said Vicki. She caught her sister's eye and raised her eyebrows.

Then, embarrassed, she realized that Marty had seen her do it.

He smiled, a thin, humorless smile. "You're welcome," he said. "Have a nice trip home." He stuck his hands in his jacket pockets and sauntered away.

Vicki shook her head. "What a piece of work."

"I don't like him," said Alaina, like a child.

"Come on," said Vicki, "before he changes his mind and comes back to haunt us."

Dace was there the next day. It was funny. She was walking toward her locker, and she thought she saw a golden head of hair. Alaina.

And then Dace was smiling down at her.

"I came to collect my thank you," he said.

Vicki tilted her chin up. Keep breathing, she told herself. Normally. "Thank you," she murmured demurely.

"I had a little more than that in mind," Dace said. He was smiling in a way that made her feel as if maybe her father was right about wearing her clothes too tight — although not for the same reasons.

"More?"

"Movie? This Saturday?"

She wasn't dizzy, she was in orbit. But from up above, where her astral self was singing "Joy to the World," she heard her earthbound self say, calmly, "Saturday. Okay. Sounds good to me. It's the least I can do. . . ."

"No," said Mr. Clements.

Vicki felt her eyes suddenly fill with tears. Damn! She'd gotten so weak lately. Stop it. "Why? He's a perfectly nice guy. At least meet him before you say no."

"You're just getting back to school. You shouldn't overexert yourself. Look at you now. I don't let you have your way about one little thing, and you're in hysterics."

"I'm *not* . . ." Hearing her voice go up, Vicki gritted her teeth. Then she said, "I'm not in hysterics. I just don't understand why I can't go out with Dace on Saturday night. I'm sixteen. I went out before, before — I went out last year!"

"That's different." Her father raised the newspaper in front of his face, his typically subtle signal that the conversation was at an end. No way it is, thought Vicki.

"What's different about it?"

The newspaper came down. "You'll do it because I say so."

"But why?"

"What about a double date?" Alan was propped

against the den door frame, his arms folded.

"What's that you said, Alan?" Father is using his my-father-the-criminal-attorney-butcher-knife glare, thought Vicki. But Alan was unmoved.

"I said what about a double date. I've got a date. Let Vicki and Jordon come along. He's all right. And I'll keep my eye on them."

Vicki waited, afraid to say anything. Finally, finally, Mr. Clements nodded slowly. "I don't know what I'm thinking of, to think you'd be any kind of a chaperone. But okay."

"All right! Alan, thanks!"

"No problem, sister dearie," said Alan, and slid out of the doorway.

Impulsively, Vicki threw her arms around her father's neck. He stiffened and drew back. Hurt, Vicki drew back, too.

"Just be home by midnight, you hear?" He raised the paper in front of him again before she could answer.

If I wear that black skirt, the really short one I got last spring, I'll never get out of the house. Too bad. I haven't even gotten to break it in.

Saturday night at last. It had been the longest week of her life. Except for the ones in the hospital. She frowned, then her thoughts veered off again.

The black jeans. Yes. And a loose sweater. She could drop the sweater off her bare shoulder when she got out of the house. And of course, her red shoes.

Sitting on the edge of her bed, wriggling her feet into the shoes, she smiled. Sexy shoes, Janet had said. But her father just thought they were feminine.

"What's the joke?" Alaina stopped in the door.

"Nothing. How do I look?" Vicki stood up and made a snake-hip movement toward her sister.

Alan had come up behind Alaina. Amazing how much alike they looked. Not just like fraternal twins. Like identical twins almost. "Nice hip action," Alan said.

Vicki gave her brother her most seductive pout. "Isn't it, though," she said.

"And what a bad little girl."

"It's when I'm best."

"You two," said Alaina indulgently.

"Hold that thought," said Alan to Vicki. "I think I hear a car."

A few minutes later she was hurrying down the stairs to open the door for Dace.

Was it legal for a guy to look as good as Dace did? Vicki stole a look at her father as she introduced Dace to him. He didn't look impressed. "Nice to meet you," he rapped out. "Have her back by twelve. Both of you."

"You can trust me," said Alan. "Can we go now? I got someone waiting. Impatiently." He turned and led the way out the door. "Nice guy, isn't he, Jordon?"

"He's got a lovely daughter," said Dace. He caught Vicki's hand in his and gave a quick squeeze as they got in the car. Alan slid into the back.

"Where to? Who's the hot date?"

"Drop me off at the corner," said Alan.

"What?" Vicki swung around to face her brother.

"Look, call it a favor. I don't want you cramping my style." Alan smiled, looking for a moment like the old Alan, her favorite sib, her best friend. Then the look was gone, replaced by the shut, watching look he always wore these days.

"All *right*!" said Dace.

"Alan," began Vicki.

"Save your appreciation. For him." Alan nodded toward Dace, then slid out of the car. "See ya. And don't forget. Cinderella gets turned into pumpkin pie at midnight."

"You like horror movies?" asked Dace.

"If someone is with me," said Vicki. "Close by."

Dace grinned. "Let's go."

They laughed all the way through. They were still laughing, sitting over pizza an hour after the movie was over.

" 'Blooood,' " moaned Dace. " 'Be he alive, or be he dead, give me some blood to spread my bread.' "

"Ugh. That was the worst. I thought all that blood would bother me, but it was so plastic."

"Yeah . . . you were brave. I bet you watched at least half of it with your eyes open."

"I liked the plot," said Vicki. "I liked the part where the guy came out of the woods in those perma-press pants."

"You liked the pants."

Vicki smiled, started to say something back, then stopped. She had the strangest sensation. Like she was being watched. She turned suddenly. But it was just kids, people she knew, on dates. Normal people, she thought. Like me.

"Something the matter?"

"Nah." Vicki shrugged, feeling foolish.

Trying to change the subject she said, "You get that way in a house full of siblings. The feeling that you should watch your back. You know?"

Dace frowned. Looked at his watch.

"Well, it's almost time, Cinderella. We gotta leave now if I'm gonna see you to your door right."

What just happened, she wondered. What did I say? But she couldn't think of how to ask, so she just smiled. Mysteriously, she hoped.

He kissed as good as he looked. Not that I have a whole lot to compare it to lately, she thought wryly. But maybe I'm going to get to make up for lost time. Then she forgot about thinking, leaning into him again, sliding her hands up under his shirt.

"Ummhmm," she sighed. Or thought she did.

It was Dace who leaned back. She expected him to say something cool. But he didn't. He put his hand up and touched her cheek. His face was shadowed.

"I had a good time," he said. "A really good time."

Before she could answer, he'd turned and headed back down the walk. She stood and watched his car drive away, stood with her back against the door after that. It was such a beautiful night. All the stars were out, looking down at her. And she was one of them. Such a beautiful, beautiful night.

And then she heard it. Soft. Low. Malicious.

Someone laughing. Laughing in the shadows somewhere nearby.

Laughing at her.

Chapter 4

"Who's that?" she said.

The laughter continued, soft, soft, a vein of sound pulsing in the night. Coming from everywhere. Coming from nowhere.

"Who's there?" she said, surprised to hear how firm and sure her voice sounded.

She wanted to step forward, to be as brave as her voice made her sound. But she found that somehow, instead, she was pressed back against the front door, fumbling for her keys with hands that were suddenly sweaty and cold.

"Who is . . ."

A hand grabbed her shoulder.

"No! NO!"

She was falling, being pulled back and down.

With a wrench she broke free and whirled around.

Her father stood there, watching her. She squinted back at him in the sudden glare of the porch light, trying to catch her breath.

"What's going on here?" He studied her, a look that said, *crazy kid.*

But she was listening to the pounding of her heart, and the eerie silence of the night.

The silence. The laughter had stopped.

"Did you hear that?" she asked.

Her father frowned. "Hear what?" Then, before she could answer, he looked past her and his frown deepened. "Where's Alan?"

"Alan?" She rubbed her hands on her pants. A mistake. Her father looked down at her legs, frowned again. He cleared his throat.

"Heeeere's Alan!"

"Alan!" Vicki swung around as Alan loped into the edge of the light from the front porch.

"Hey, I told you I was just going to drop off my date . . . I told you I'd be right back. Didn't I?"

"C'mon then," her father said. "It's late."

He stepped back, and Alan and Vicki walked in past him and started up the stairs to their rooms.

"Alan," whispered Vicki. He kept going.

"Alan," she hissed.

"What?" he said, stopping at the top of the stairs.

"Did you hear anything?"

"Hear anything what? When?"

"Just now. Outside?"

Alan shrugged.

"Someone was out there. They were . . . they were laughing."

"C'mon, Vicki, what're you talking about?"

"Good-*night*."

Vicki and Alan turned. Their father was still standing in the hall, staring up at them. He raised his arm and looked pointedly at his watch.

"Right," said Alan. "Night, Pops. Night, Vicki."

"Good-night," said Vicki. She looked down at her father. He looked so normal, so All-American, standing there in the hall in that funky old plaid bathrobe. So solid. So fatherly.

"Night," she repeated softly, and turned and went to bed.

By the next Monday afternoon she was ragged. She hadn't seen Dace, and Janet was mired in the art room on her project. And everywhere she went, she seemed to run into Caddie. How could someone who was sly and calculating be so obvious?

"Buy a vowel, Caddie," she muttered, and turned off into the girls' down the hall. She pushed open the door to one of the stalls and pulled the seat down. She propped her feet up against the door and, fishing around in her pack, found what she was looking for at last.

She'd just gotten the cigarette lit when the door opened.

Damn, she thought, spitting frantically on her fingers and trying to pinch the cigarette out.

Then Janet's voice came from outside the stall door.

"Vicki? Vicki, are you in there?"

"Janet? What'r'you, following me? Aren't you supposed to be doing your arts and crafts?"

Vicki bumped the door open with her feet, and Janet leaned against it, cradling her sling bag in her arms. She let Vicki's putdown slide — almost. "Hey, Vick! Since when did you smoke?"

"Since when is it any of your business," Vicki snapped.

"Since anytime these last sixteen years or so." Janet held up one finger. "Blood is thicker than water, right?"

Vicki suddenly flashed on the memory: the two of them, seven years old, eyes closed, trying to get up enough courage to be blood sisters. But neither of them wanted to go first, sticking the needle in their fingers. Then suddenly, Janet had squeezed her eyes shut and done it. So Vicki had done it, too. And then they had both started crying.

"I'm sorry," said Vicki. She looked at the cigarette. "And you're right, I don't smoke. I don't know why I bought these. I don't know what's gotten into me these days . . . ugh."

She stood up, flipped the cigarette in the toilet, and flushed it. "Let's go," she said.

Janet grinned impishly. "I confess, I did follow you. I mean, I couldn't believe we were stuck at my uncle's all day and he wouldn't let me have one little bitty long distance phone call. I mean it wasn't that far. . . . So tell me about Dace. What was it like." She made a descriptive gesture with her hands that made Vicki laugh and gasp, almost choking.

Pleased, Janet nodded. "I knew it," she said. "Tell me."

But as they came out of the girls', before Vicki could regain her composure, Caddie Melville blocked her path.

"Well, if it isn't the Bobbsey Twins," she sneered.

Janet drew herself up, and gave Caddie a once-over.

Caddie's sneer stayed in place. "You shouldn't

try that move," she told Janet. "You haven't got the build for it."

Incredibly, Janet's face flushed. Vicki couldn't believe it. Since when did Janet ever let anyone, especially someone like Caddie, get under her skin?

"You know what, Caddie," said Vicki.

And Caddie fell for it. "What?"

"You're a jerk," said Vicki.

Caddie pressed her narrow lips together furiously. Her round face mottled red.

Vicki pressed her advantage. "You shouldn't turn that color. You haven't got the looks for it."

She turned and walked away, with Janet half a step behind, leaving Caddie standing there.

When they were out of hearing, Vicki stole a glance at Janet. Janet's head was down, her normally bouncy step practically a shuffle.

"Hey," said Vicki. "Don't let her get to you."

"Why is it," said Janet, "that the big stupid ones know your weaknesses best?"

"Huh? That crack about your figure? Forget it. You've got a great figure."

"I'm fat."

"I should be so fat in the same places."

"Some people think Caddie's sexy."

"Some people have no taste. You know what, Caddie's just jealous of you. She's paranoid and insecure. She's a . . . would-be has-been, nothing on top, and . . . nothing on top of that!" Vicki tapped her own forehead solemnly.

Janet looked up then, and smiled a little. "Pretty pitiful, Vick."

"She's pretty pitiful. Even Alaina the soft heart

wouldn't let her into the Deltas. Remember that whole scene? Caddie was outta control. Made herself look really bad."

"Yeah . . . again. Of course, I might not make it in the Deltas either," Janet added thoughtfully.

"You will."

The bounce began to return to Janet's step. "On my charm. And my connections. I mean, Alaina can't turn down a sister's blood sister, right?"

"You don't even like Alaina. And if you asked me, I think the Deltas are a bunch of twisted sisters. Why do you want to — ?"

"Because," Janet interrupted. "Anyway, know what I think? Caddie's just using me to get at you. Everyone knows she'd do anything for Marty."

"Anything?" teased Vicki.

Janet laughed aloud now. "Anything," she declared. "Only she can't get him to ask!"

"Great. With friends like you who needs enemies?"

Janet grinned at Vicki, and for a moment Vicki saw, behind the big brown eyes and sleek cap of hair and outspoken ways, the funny little girl who had always been her best friend.

"Hey," said Janet. "My friends are your friends."

"And my enemies are your enemies," Vicki answered.

It was part of the old best friends ritual, the solemn oath of blood sisterhood.

But what if I told Janet about last night, about the laughing stuff, wondered Vicki. What would she say about that? Would she believe me?

Or would she think I was crazy?

Chapter 5

It was a bright and sunny morning. The birds were singing. The air was fresh and cool. She could almost taste it.

Fly girl, thought Vicki, heading into the front door of Amelia Earhart like she owned the place. And maybe I do, she thought. After all, my parents are the taxpaying public, right? And then she thought: Hey, I'm the taxpaying public, too.

She was wearing her high-tops today, with layers of socks and layers of T-shirts and a sweater, and black skinpants and a demure knee-length pleated skirt. As soon as she got to the girls' she was going to lose the skirt.

The girls' was dense with smoke today. "Help, help, fire, fire," said Vicki, swimming through it to a stall.

"Stick it," offered a voice from one of the others.

Vicki laughed, and shimmied out of the skirt. A few minutes later she hit the halls again, the skirt condensed into a neat roll at the bottom of her backpack.

And there was Dace, like magic.

He checked her out. She stepped back to give him a good look, and then made a point of checking him out, too. His jeans were almost as tight as her skinpants, and worn soft in all the right places.

"Sweet," she said.

"Pretty to look at, nicer to hold," he answered, and fell into step beside her. "Can I hold anything of yours?"

And then, dammit, she started to blush.

"Like, you know, your books or something?" he added gravely.

She laughed. She couldn't help it. If you could see me now, Dad, she thought.

"That good, huh?" asked Dace. "So let's keep the good times rolling. What're you doing Saturday night?"

She laughed again, and said, "I asked you first."

He smiled down at her then and she stopped laughing. She might have stopped breathing. And she definitely was not walking on the plain old hall floor of Amelia Earhart High.

High. Higher. Highest. She was flying.

Now Dace was leaning over just a little, just close enough for her to think about what it would be like to kiss him here, now, to run her hands over those jeans, to . . .

"I'm going out," he whispered. "I hope. With this incredible girl."

And then they both were laughing, and she'd never been so happy in her whole life.

"*Another* date? God, Vicki, this is serious!"

Janet was sitting next to Vicki in the girls' locker

room, lacing up her gym shoes. "What luck, girl!"

"Luck!" Vicki pretended to be insulted. "Luck! What about my incredible charm, my great sense of humor, my fascinating good looks?"

Janet didn't say anything for a second, struggling with her laces. Then she looked up, her face red from exertion. "That, too," she said. "Do you think he'll ask you to homecoming?"

"Homecoming!" Lolly popped out, seemingly from one of the lockers. "Ooh! Who has a date to homecoming already? I mean, I have my dress practically picked out, but I haven't got a date yet."

Janet stood up. "C'mon. Ms. Hazelett will be down here waling on us if we don't hurry up."

"I bet even Alaina doesn't have a date yet," said Lolly, looking at Vicki hopefully. "Does she?"

"Alaina's not dating much this year," said Vicki. "Since Craig Waring went off to college."

"Right. Brokenhearted Alaina." Janet hooked her arm through Lolly's and practically dragged her out of the locker room. Vicki shook her head, and finished tying her other gym shoe. The one-minute warning whistle sounded faintly overhead.

"Coming, coming," she muttered, fishing around in her locker for the band to tie her hair back. There.

It was nice of Janet to head Lolly off like that, but she didn't need her to run interference. The way I feel today, thought Vicki, nothing Lolly or anyone could do could bother me. She slammed the locker and bounded for the door, twisting her hair back as she ran.

Half an hour later, staggering toward the showers, she had to admit she was wrong.

"What happened?" gasped Janet. "I thought we were just gonna play a little friendly basketball."

"That was until Hazelett put Caddie on the other team." Janet pulled off her shirt and wiped her face. "You wouldn't think someone as big as Melville would be able to get *both* kidneys on someone as short as I am."

"At least Hazelett called it a foul. She was letting Melville get away with murder."

"Everyone does. She's spoiled rotten. Anyway you're lucky. You've got an excuse to sit out part of these brawls . . . "

"Yeah, it must be nice to be treated special because you're practically a cripple now," said a voice behind them.

Janet gave a little gasp, then snapped, "Your towel's slipping, Caddie."

Vicki didn't even turn her head. "Melville. Melville," she mused. "Wasn't that the name of a whale . . . no, I'm sorry. That was the author. The whale's name was Moby. Moby *Dick*."

"You've got problems, Vicki, you know? Big, sick problems. You and your girlfriend." Caddie pushed angrily past them.

"Oh, go sniff old socks," muttered Janet. "Vicki, I didn't mean you were lucky to be in the accident . . . I mean . . ."

"Don't worry about it." Will it never end, she thought, stepping into the shower.

She turned on the shower and slid under. It felt so good. She took her time. When she got out, the showers were empty.

"Janet?" she said. No answer. I hope I didn't

miss the bell, she thought, and hurried toward her locker.

Lolly and a couple of other girls were still in front of the mirrors, repairing their makeup. "That was some game, huh," Lolly was saying as Vicki came around the corner.

"Way to go, Lolly," said Vicki.

"Thank you," said Lolly seriously. Lolly was a surprisingly good basketball player. Must have something to do with an excess of instincts, thought Vicki.

Janet, who was dressed now, was sprawled melodramatically across the bench at the end of the row of lockers, trying to get the zipper up on her jeans.

"I'm too weak," she moaned.

"Is *that* the problem?" asked Vicki.

"Absolutely," said Janet, outraged. She gave the zipper one last, finally successful tug and sat up. "See?"

Janet snatched her backpack out of the locker she shared with Vicki and slammed the door.

"What's the rush?" asked Vicki.

"Art calls," Janet said over her shoulder. "See ya later."

"See ya," called Vicki. She smiled to herself. Papier mâché waits for no woman, I guess, she thought. She wished Janet would let her see what her art project was. But Janet was being very mysterious about the whole thing — uncharacteristically modest, even.

The locker room sounded like it had emptied out completely now. It was strangely peaceful. Still feeling loose from the shower and, not that she'd ever tell anybody, pretty good about holding her own on the basketball court that day, she pulled on her clothes.

She looked at her watch.

"Great," she said aloud, and leaning over, yanked out her backpack and her shoes. She slung the backpack onto the bench beside her and jerked her hightops on, fast.

And jumped up, and fell down, writhing and screaming on the floor.

Chapter 6

"*Nononononononono!*"

Her voice spiraled up and up against the institutional colored walls. She clawed at her ankles, fell back, her feet in the air, kicking, screaming.

Doors slammed. Footsteps raced toward her as she arched in the air. One shoe came off and sailed against the locker.

Ms. Hazelett ran around the corner, followed by Lolly, and Caddie, and half a dozen others.

"Get it off, get it off," she screamed, pushing her stockinged foot against her other shoe, kicking out at Ms. Hazelett.

Then the other shoe came off and fell to the floor.

Scrambling backwards on her hands and heels, she crashed against the lockers.

"Get them away from me, get them off," she howled.

"Vicki . . . Vicki, calm down," Ms. Hazelett had her shoulders now, gripping them tightly. "Listen to me. Calm down. It's all right."

Vicki gave a little gasp.

"Vicki!"

She focused on her teacher's face.

"It was . . . it was . . ."

"It's okay now," said Ms. Hazelett.

"Ms. Hazelett," said Lolly.

"Here," said Ms. Hazelett, "sit up now. You — Lolly, go get a glass of water."

"Ms. Hazelett," said Lolly.

"Now," said Ms. Hazelett.

Lolly hurried off, her flat-bottom shoes sliding over the cement floors, whisper, whisper, whisper.

The others were whispering too, the girls standing in the locker room.

Lolly came back and handed Ms. Hazelett the water, stepping carefully around the shoes.

"Drink this," commanded Ms. Hazelett.

Vicki obeyed. When she'd finished it, she tried to smile. "I'm okay," she whispered.

"What happened?" asked her teacher.

"It was . . . I put on . . ."

"Ms. Hazelett!" Lolly's voice thinned up to a shriek.

"What is it, Lolly!"

"Her shoes. Vicki's shoes. There are roaches crawling out of them. Hundreds and hundreds of *roaches!*"

"I'm all right now," said Vicki.

"Are you sure?" Ms. Hazelett's shrewd eyes narrowed. "You have any idea who might have done this?"

"No." Vicki sat up carefully. The room stayed in place. She took a deep breath. "It was just some dumb joke, I guess."

Ms. Hazelett waited.

"I mean, why would anyone do anything like that, except as a joke."

"I didn't find it funny. Did you?"

"No way." Vicki tried a shrug. "But I guess some people would."

"The question," said Ms. Hazelett, "is who?"

She paused again, then went on when Vicki didn't volunteer any more information. "Vicki. Is everything okay? At home? Here at school?"

"Of course it is!" Vicki looked up, hoping her surprise would look like indignation. "Why wouldn't it be?"

"You tell me," said Ms. Hazelett.

"There's nothing to tell! I'm fine. I wish people would quit asking me all these questions. I wish they'd quit treating me like I'm . . ." She stopped.

Ms. Hazelett pounced. "Like you're what?"

Like I'm crazy. "Like I'm some kind of invalid. I'm fine. And it's no big deal. Just some lowlife's idea of a joke, that's all."

Ms. Hazelett waited a minute longer, then scribbled in her notebook. "If anything comes up, if you find out anything about this, let me know."

"Yes." Vicki stood up.

Ms. Hazelett ripped out the piece of paper. "Here's your pass to the next class."

"Thank you."

Her teacher's voice stopped her at the door. "Vicki. I think there's more to this than you're telling . . . maybe more than you know."

"I've got to get to class," said Vicki.

"Take it easy," said Ms. Hazelett.

* * *

By the time she got to her next class, it was all over the school. Thank goodness it was the last class of the day. Too bad it had to be biology. She sat there staring straight ahead while the teacher talked about amoebas and flagellates, or some such thing. She tried to ignore the way everyone watched her, and whispered.

Who, she kept thinking. Who hates me so much?

Caddie Melville had sure been on the spot fast. Was it possible that Caddie hated her so much? Just over Marty? How could anybody be that much under Marty's spell? Anybody with any sense, she amended.

But Caddie wasn't dumb. Primitive maybe, but not dumb. But then, Marty has that kind of animal appeal. Even she'd fallen for it for a little while herself.

Then she remembered her conversation in the gym with Janet. Alaina's sorority. The Deltas — juniors and seniors only, and a very select group at that — were the best sorority in school, if you liked that sort of thing. Vicki didn't. She wasn't about to waste her time on making nice with a bunch of clones when she could be having fun.

On the other hand, having Alaina in the Deltas made it a lot easier for Vicki to blow it off that way, she had to admit. Let Alaina be sweet and smiling and golden, one of the original social graces. However, Alaina was also capable of being stubborn about a few things. And the sorority was one of the few things important enough to Alaina for Alaina to get stubborn about.

Alaina had a lot of influence, too. Her sorority sisters did what she told them to do. If Alaina wasn't speaking to someone, none of the Deltas was. Sometimes it was a little spooky how much power Alaina had over them.

Caddie had wanted in. But someone had said no. It only took one vote.

Vicki had always assumed the decision had been Alaina's. But had it? And had Caddie found out?

Vicki shook her head.

Don't be ridiculous, she thought. Caddie's not that subtle. She wouldn't go after you to get at Alaina.

Then she remembered Janet's words: Caddie's out to get at you through me. Funny how Janet didn't like Caddie *or* Alaina. Two such opposite people. Yet they seemed to inspire the same disdain in Janet.

Funny, too, how Janet would want to be one of the Deltas when she felt that way about Alaina. Of course, like Janet said, I have some influence with Alaina myself, thought Vicki wryly. So that lets Janet out as a suspect.

And she immediately felt ashamed of herself for even suspecting her best friend. Sometimes, she felt as if Janet was the only person in the whole world she could really trust.

She shook her head again to clear her thoughts. It was just a joke, she told herself. Just a dumb, stupid joke.

Chapter 7

"Caddie," insisted Janet.

"Maybe." Vicki was talking softly, pressed into the corner of the hall at her house so no one could hear. She knew from past experience — from listening to Alaina's conversations when she was a kid — how conversations from the phone in the front hall traveled up the stairs.

Just another example of her old-fashioned father. Of course, he wasn't too old-fashioned to have a separate phone in his study. And another one in the master bedroom. Just too into power to ditch the one in the front hall and get a cordless. Or at least let Alan and Alaina and Vicki have their own line upstairs.

Too bad, thought Vicki. He doesn't know what he's missing. Then he could shout all the way up the stairs for us to get off the phone.

"It has to be Caddie." Janet was persisting.

"Why do you keep saying it was Caddie?" asked Vicki. "It could have been anybody. It's not like the locker rooms are hard to get into. Or that our combination is any way a big secret. We've had the same locker for two years. And think of all the people who've had that locker before us."

"True." Janet was quiet for a moment. "I guess anyone *can* get in there. Remember when the guys team tried that major crude panty raid one gym period?" She giggled.

"And remember Ms. Hazelett crashing the male sanctity of the boys locker room to get them back?" Vicki giggled softly, too. "I wish I had seen it."

"Vicki!" said Janet in mock horror.

"Pretty rude of them to mix the underwear up with all those old socks. . . ."

"You didn't actually fish yours out, then wear them home, did you?" Janet cried.

"No! I went without . . ."

"Whoa, whoa . . . so if it wasn't Caddie . . . wait a minute." The laughter went out of Janet's voice. "Wait a minute."

Vicki heard her father's footsteps. "Is someone on the phone?"

"Maybe it wasn't Caddie. And maybe it wasn't meant for you!"

"What do you mean?"

"Vicki, is that you out there on the phone?"

Vicki said, "It's me, Dad. I'm getting off. Janet, what do you mean?"

"I mean, we share that locker. Why should someone be out to get you? What if it is someone who is out to get *me*?"

Rutland Clement's shadow fell across Vicki.

"That's crazy," said Vicki.

"Vicki," said her father.

"What if it *is* me?"

"It's *not*."

"How do you know?"

"Trust me. Listen, I gotta go."

Vicki hung up the phone, hard, and jumped to her feet.

"Who was that?" asked her father.

"Don't I have any privacy around here?" Vicki shouted. Her father took an involuntary step back, surprise on his face. "It was Jack the Ripper, okay? Take your old telephone!" She stormed upstairs to her room and slammed the door behind her.

She lay across the bed, waiting for her father to come upstairs and let her have it for being impertinent. But he never came. Weird. After awhile, she calmed down. Think, she told herself. Get a grip on yourself.

You know it's not Janet they're after. . . . They? They? You are getting paranoid, she told herself.

But I know it's not Janet. It's me.

She remembered the soft, menacing laughter.

No one else heard it, she told herself. Not even Alan, and he was right there.

Alan?

No way. It couldn't be Alan. Why would it be?

But Alan had changed, everybody said so. Had he changed enough to want to do this to her? To haunt her? To try to drive her crazy?

And then out of nowhere, she thought of Marty. Super stud. Super ego. Was he trying to pay her back for dumping him?

Yeah, right, she thought. He hasn't even noticed he's been dumped.

Then she suddenly remembered that Marty had PE at the same time. Marty Hormone? Had his hormones really gotten out of control?

But if it were true — who would believe her? And how could she prove it?

Marty. The thought of him made her skin crawl.

Breathe. Breathe. Each breath was a horrible struggle. Her lungs were on fire. This was how it felt to smother. To drown. She was drowning in pain. She opened her eyes and the world was red. Drowning in blood.

No. It was a nightmare. She really was awake. In her own room. "Aaah." She tried to speak. And couldn't. Tried to breathe. And couldn't.

Something was over her mouth, holding her down. Killing her.

Someone was in her room, on her bed, smothering her to death.

The nightmare was real.

"Aaahh." The scream was trapped in her raw throat, and then a soft voice whispered, "Shh. It's okay."

Where have I heard those words before, thought Vicki incoherently.

"Shhh. Vicki. It's me."

Alaina. Her sister.

"Shhh." Slowly Alaina lifted her hand.

"Wh-what happened?"

"You were having a nightmare. I could hear you all the way in my room. I came in to wake you up . . . so Mom and Dad wouldn't hear."

"Oh, Alaina." Vicki struggled up and fell heavily against Alaina's shoulder. "Oh God, Alaina."

"It was what happened today, wasn't it," said Alaina.

"What's going on?" sobbed Vicki. "What's going on?"

"It was just a joke, just a sick joke." Alaina's voice seemed to go up. "Some pervert's idea of fun."

A shadow moved in the half-open door of Vicki's room. Vicki gasped.

"Who's there?" she croaked. "Who is it?"

"Relax." Alan's dry, sardonic tone was clear even in his whisper. "I heard the kickup, I came around, that's all."

"You heard," repeated Alaina. "How? Your room is all the way at the other end of the house."

"I'm a light sleeper," said Alan.

Alaina put her arm around Vicki, and the two sisters sat, looking at the shadowy figure in the doorway.

It's creepy, thought Vicki suddenly. The way he stands there, watching, waiting . . .

"I'm . . . I'm fine now, Alan," she said aloud. "It was just a dream."

"Well, don't let it bug you," said Alan. "That was a joke, Vicki. Get it?"

"Oh, Alan," whispered Vicki.

"Good-night, Alan," said Alaina.

He stood there for a moment longer, and then he was gone, his soft footsteps fading into the darkness.

Vicki felt Alaina relax like a rag doll against her.

Why is she so afraid of Alan? she wondered.

And then she realized how odd it was to have Alaina that close to her. Alaina, who never touched anybody. She really *was* afraid of Alan.

Recognizing that, Vicki realized something even more horrible, as bad as her worst nightmare. Something worse than the creeps that Marty gave her. Something worse than the revulsion that Caddie raised in her gut.

The brother Vicki had loved and trusted all her life, the brother she admired, wasn't the same brother. Ever since the night he'd been driving the car when she'd had the accident, he'd changed.

And now, she didn't trust him anymore.

She was afraid of him, too.

Chapter 8

"I'm the one. I know I am," moaned Janet.

"Janet. Stop! We've been over it and over it. What possible reason could anyone have for playing that kind of perverted trick on you?" Vicki was sick of hearing about it, sick of the way Janet was sticking to her like glue. Sometimes, sisterhood could go too far.

Janet did not look convinced. Instead, she said stubbornly, for about the thousandth time, "What reason would anyone have to do that to you?"

For about the thousandth time Vicki thought of the laughter in the dark, and echoed Janet's words in her thoughts: Why? Who hated her so much?

"Look," Janet went on, "unless you did it yourself, how can you *know* it wasn't meant for me?"

Vicki lost her temper. "I just know, okay? But if you want it to be you, go ahead, be my guest!"

She must have said it louder than she thought, because heads turned in the hall and inside the math classroom where she was headed.

The two girls stopped and turned to face each other. Then Janet shrugged, a funny little smile on her lips, and said, "Hey, I didn't mean you'd do something like that yourself, you know."

"I didn't think you did," Vicki answered coolly.

"Hey, it's over, right? Let's forget it."

"That's what *I'm* trying to do, okay?" And shaking Janet off, she turned and went into her class, trying to ignore the looks she was getting, trying to think about Dace, about the weekend ahead that they were planning to spend together. Now that she and Dace were getting serious, she wasn't paying as much attention to Janet. And when she was, Janet was getting on her nerves.

She felt close to Dace like she had never felt close to anyone before. She was comfortable just being with him. He made her feel safe, good, beautiful. Dace really did help her forget what had happened.

And pain that she was being these days, Janet helped in another way, a real way. When Vicki was complaining about how strict her father was, how he wouldn't let her go out with Dace alone at night so that the two of them were stuck doing kid stuff in the afternoons, (although she'd had fun on the swings with him, out on the deserted playground at the elementary school next door — not to mention doing a little tandem sliding), Janet had said, "Let's double up. Your father would go for that, I bet."

And amazingly enough, he had.

Vicki leaned back against Dace's arm in the booth in Nick's restaurant. Janet and her date of the week were cutting up with some of the other cheerleaders and their dates. She looked up to find Dace looking down at her.

"Hi," she said.

"Hi." They smiled at each other.

She leaned back again, still smiling, and caught Janet's eye. Janet looked thoughtful, just for a moment maybe a little sad. Then she flashed her dimples at Vicki.

"Ooh ooh," she said softly, and turned back to join in the raucous laughter at some disgusting jock joke.

Janet is such a party animal, thought Vicki affectionately. But not me. Not anymore.

"Tell me?" Dace said softly against her ear.

"Tell you what?" she asked, turning her head. "What do you want . . .?"

His mouth brushed hers. "Everything . . ."

Maybe, Vicki thought, forgetting where she was, forgetting who she was, maybe one day I will.

Dace was too good. His kisses almost brought her low, the next time they met after school.

"Excuse me."

The words were polite but the voice wasn't. It was steely and ice-cold.

Vicki moaned a little and half-turned her head, her mouth still bruised from Dace's lips.

Then her eyes focused.

The principal!

Dace saw Principal Sewell at the same instant. He grew stiffer against her, but he took his time leaning back.

"Hello," he said.

Vicki could feel the hot blood running up her cheeks. Hastily she tried to tuck her shirttail in and push back her disheveled hair.

Principal Sewell ignored him.

"Public displays of affection — *if* you can call what you were doing affection — are strictly prohibited on school grounds."

"We're sorry," drawled Dace. "It won't happen again."

Vicki glanced at him nervously. Somehow, she thought that was the wrong tone to take with the principal.

"We're sorry," she said, trying to look sincere, still pressed against the wall. Dace hadn't leaned far enough back for her to straighten up.

He did now. "Sorry?" he asked, looking at her. She felt her blush spread down her neck.

Before she could answer, the principal snapped, "You, young man, are excused. You," she fixed her glinting green eyes on Vicki, "come with me, young lady."

"W-what?"

"NOW." The principal turned and marched down the hall.

"But — "

Principal Sewell wheeled. "School is over for the day, Mr. Jordon. You are on the premises after hours without permission. If you don't want further trouble, I suggest you leave now."

"Excuse me," muttered Dace.

"Go on," said Vicki. "I'll be fine."

As Dace gave Vicki one quick, unreadable look,

Principal Sewell sneered, "I wouldn't count on it if I were you, miss."

Vicki was shaking. "No one, *no one* has ever talked to me like that before," she said, trying to keep her voice under control.

She was standing in front of Principal Sewell's desk. The principal was sitting on the other side, looking like the combination of a nun and a mortician in her black suit and white blouse.

"Perhaps it is time someone did," said Principal Sewell. "The point is, I will not tolerate that kind of behavior in my school. It is after hours, and you shouldn't be here, much less here alone engaged in the kind of behavior in which I found you."

"What? We were just — "

"That's enough." The principal held up her hand. "It was lewd and disgusting, and I advise you not to let it happen again!" She pointed to the phone on her desk. "Call your parents, and have them come to pick you up."

"What? What for?" Vicki couldn't believe her ears.

"Do what I say," said the principal.

The woman was demented. No question about it. Glaring, Vicki picked up the phone and punched the digits.

"Hello," she said.

"At the sound of the tone, the time will be . . ."

"Mom, it's me. Vicki. Yes, I'm at school. . . ."

"The weather for this evening . . ."

"Yes. Could you come pick me up? I'll be on the steps. . . . Ten minutes?"

"Beeeep."

" 'Bye."

She hung up and looked back at the principal. "Did you want to talk to her?"

The principal shook her head. "I assume you can find your way out of the school?"

It's one of the first things I learned, Vicki thought, but she only said, "Yes."

"Don't dawdle."

The interview was over.

Still steaming, Vicki slammed out the front door. It fell shut behind her with a sound like a prison scene from a movie. Yeah, right, thought Vicki. Students in chains.

It was later than she thought. The orange ball of the sun had dropped to tree level, and the air had the brisk tang of early autumn. Vicki would have thought it was a beautiful night — if she hadn't been so blindingly angry.

Demented, she told herself. Sex-crazed old woman. With a filthy mind. She wants lewd, I'll give her lewd. . . .

She loped down the stairs, turned, and headed across the parking lot. She'd take the shortcut across the elementary school playground and be home before dark.

Crossing the playground, she felt her fury gradually abate. A smile came to her lips as she remembered the afternoon she and Dace had spent there.

Good thing that old bag didn't see us here. God knows what she would have made of that. . . .

She gave one of the swings a little push as she went by, and left it creaking hopefully behind her.

As she reached the bridge over the culvert at the back of the playground, she saw the streetlights come on up ahead.

Enough of this, she thought. I'd better hurry. She picked up her pace and trotted over the bridge.

She was almost across it when she heard the footsteps behind her.

No way, she thought. You're imagining it.

Still, she walked a little faster into the shadows of the sidewalk that led between the back fences of two houses, and out to the street.

The footsteps kept up.

She threw a quick, blind look over her shoulder.

Nothing. Only shadows.

I won't run, she thought. The street is just ahead. I can scream. People would hear me.

You're imagining things.

Like you imagined the laughter?

No. That was real. This . . .

Her heart was pounding so loud now she couldn't hear anything at all. She hurried on toward the edge of the light. Trying not to run, not to show how afraid she was. Just a little further. Just a little further to go toward safety and reality and life.

She was almost there.

But the footsteps had gotten there before her.

She saw the shoes first. Red shoes.

And then the feet.

And the bloody stumps of ankles where the legs should have been.

She began to scream.

She turned around and ran back into the darkness.

Chapter 9

Hands caught her shirt. A ripping sound. Screaming wildly, she swung her backpack around and connected.

"Uh! Hey. Hey, Vicki. . . . Hey, chill, will you?"

"A-Alan?" She shuddered to a stop and looked down. "You tore my shirt," she said, irrelevantly.

"Take my jacket. Now, what is going on?"

"It . . . they . . ." She looked back over her shoulder at the shadowy arch of the bridge. "Oh, Alan."

"That tells me a lot," said Alan. He took the backpack from her and looped the strap over his arm. He took her other arm and folded it under his.

"Listen, it's getting late. The paternal unit is going to be a little upset if we don't get a move on."

"No!"

"What?"

"I can't . . . I can't go back over the bridge. I can't go back *there*."

Alan said, "Cut to the chase. *What* are you talking about?"

Strangely enough, Alan's tone had a calming effect. If he could be so matter-of-fact, so could she. She took a deep breath, and told him.

Alan eyes widened for just an instant. Then his cool, imperturbable mask slipped back into place. "Stumps of feet in your red shoes? Vicki, aren't you awful young to be getting a foot fetish?"

Fury finished erasing her terror. "I know what I saw!"

"Then let's go take a look," said Alan.

"Wait." Vicki tried to pull her arm free, but Alan held tight. She stumbled. "Hey."

Alan kept going. Their footsteps sounded hollowly on the old bridge. The dark had filled the culvert below them.

"Hey!" Vicki jerked her arm against Alan's grasp, and this time his hold loosened. She crashed against the railing. She had the sickening sensation of falling, falling toward the river of darkness below.

"No!" she gasped, "N — "

Then she had Alan's arm, and righted herself.

"Relax, will you?" Alan sounded annoyed.

She straightened up, and let go of his arm again. He was going to think she really was crazy.

"You'll see," she muttered.

In spite of her resolution not to give Alan any more ammunition to use against her, her steps lagged as they approached the circle of light from the street lamp. Alan didn't seem to notice. He strode forward and stopped.

"Where are these monster feet?" he asked.

"Right there," she said from behind him.

"Right where?"

"Right *there*." She stepped up beside Alan and pointed.

She was pointing at nothing — an empty stretch of grass beside an empty sidewalk.

"They were here. I know they were. *I'm telling the truth!*" Her voice didn't sound like her own. Her voice didn't even sound human. "Alan, it's true. It's true . . ."

"Calm down," said Alan. "If you say you saw it, you saw it."

"You don't believe me, do you?" said Vicki.

"Get a grip. It doesn't matter whether I believe you or not, does it? If you believe it's true, that's what matters . . ."

"Don't try that psychobabble on me! I was in the hospital, remember? I know what it means. What you're saying, in English, is you don't believe me!"

Ignoring her outburst, Alan said, "Listen, we've got to get home, or we're going to be in big trouble."

"*I* am, you mean," she said, momentarily diverted. "I'm the one who's got all the rules now."

"Don't be melodramatic," said Alan. "We're all supposed to be on time for dinner. You, me, Alaina, the works. We'll talk about this when we get home."

Vicki stopped. "No!"

"Will you come on . . . no what?"

"No, we will not talk about it when we get home."

Alan shrugged and kept walking.

"Alan. Alan! Promise me you won't tell anybody about this! If you do tell, I'll swear you're lying."

Alan half turned. She could see his profile. Was he frowning? No, it was a trick of the shadowy light. His face was as blank as ever.

She waited for him to argue, waited for him to tell her she was wrong.

But he only said, softly, "So that's how you want to play . . . well, suit yourself." He started walking again.

She ran to catch up.

"Alan?"

He didn't answer.

"Alan, I'm going to trust you on this."

He didn't say anything. They walked home in silence, each of them alone with their thoughts.

They were just in time for dinner, heading straight to the table through the back door. Vicki expected the usual grilling from her father. But he didn't say anything; probably, thought Vicki, because she was with Alan. Her father trusted Alan.

Vicki remembered her own words: Alan, I'm going to trust you. . . .

Still, she argued with herself, if Alan had been the one who had left her shoes like that, would he have tried to persuade her to talk about it? Wouldn't he have wanted her to keep quiet about it?

Or maybe that's why he tried to get her to talk — to conceal his guilt. Maybe he was gambling on her desire to seem normal at any cost.

No. Not Alan. She trusted Alan. Didn't she?

She looked up to see her mother studying her, a little frown between her eyebrows. Vicki forced herself to smile.

Meanwhile her father was concentrating on the roast beef, which was very rare. Just the way he liked it.

"Perfect," he said. The way he said it, Vicki

thought, sounded more like a rating than a compliment.

She took the plate he handed her and put it in front of her. Her father had cut her meat from the outside, so it wasn't as rare. But it was still bloody.

Gravy, she told herself. Not blood, gravy. If I say anything, they'll think I'm nuts.

The gravy oozed over into her mashed potatoes. She forced her eyes up.

She picked up her knife, her fork. Without looking at her plate, she cut, and put the food in her mouth. Cut and chewed. Cut and chewed.

She didn't eat it all, but she must have eaten enough. No one said anything when dinner was over, and she took her plate into the kitchen. She put it on the counter, still without looking at it.

"May I be excused?" she asked, coming back into the dining room.

"No dessert?" her mother asked.

"Can I have it later? I've . . . I've got a ton of homework."

"Well . . ." Her mother hesitated.

Unexpectedly, her father nodded approvingly. "Good," he said. "Homework before dessert. Good priorities."

Her mother smiled. "Dessert later then."

Vicki felt like her own smile was some horrible grimace, but no one seemed to notice. "Thanks," she rasped, and went to her room.

Her closet door was half open. She stopped, afraid to go any closer. What if her shoes weren't there? Or what if they were . . . with those feet still in them?

Don't be silly, she told herself. They couldn't have been real feet. They were fake. Halloween feet . . . weren't they?

She didn't know how long she'd stood there, staring at her partially open closet door. She lost track of time, of where she was. It was hearing footsteps in the hall behind her that propelled her across the room. She reached out and jerked the closet door open just as Alaina spoke her name.

"Vicki."

Vicki stared down. Her red shoes were there, neatly aligned, just where she'd left them.

"Vicki?"

Slowly Vicki turned. "Alaina. Come on in."

"Is everything okay, Vicki?"

Vicki closed her closet door, folded her arms, and leaned against it. "What do you mean?"

"I mean, I heard about that awful practical joke in gym. Have you — are you having trouble at school?"

"It was just a joke," said Vicki. "Nothing to it."

"Are you sure?"

"Yes!" Vicki spoke more sharply than she'd intended. Careful, she told herself. Control. "Yes," she repeated in a softer voice. "I'm sure."

"You know," said Alaina, almost to herself, "it's not wrong to have problems. It's human. What's wrong is to hold it all inside. If you do that, you hurt yourself."

Vicki rolled her eyes. First Alan, now Alaina. Alaina would be a great shrink. She was always trying to help people, always trying to take care of them. Sometimes Vicki admired her older sister for it. Sometimes she found it sick-making.

Like now.

"Alaina, don't worry, okay?"

Alaina went on, reflectively, as if she'd forgotten Vicki was there. "You know, people look at me, they think I'm some kind of shining example. But I'm not. It's just as hard for me. Sometimes harder, always trying to be perfect, always trying to live up to high standards."

"Spare me," muttered Vicki.

Looking up, Alaina gave Vicki a wry grin. "Yeah," she said ruefully. "It makes you uncomfortable, doesn't it, when I talk like a dweeb, instead of your homecoming queen sister . . . ?"

Vicki opened her mouth, started to give Alaina grief, then stopped. Maybe there was a little, a very little truth in what Alaina said. Maybe she needed to cut Alaina a little slack. She closed her mouth and shrugged noncommittally.

Alaina softly laughed. "You look just like Alan. . . ."

They were both quiet for a minute, then Alaina said, "Just one more thing. Dace is — "

Vicki stiffened. "What about Dace?"

"Nothing. I mean, he's a great guy. But you know, don't feel like you're all alone. He's had his share of problems, too."

"What are you talking about?"

"He hasn't told you? Well, it's not a secret exactly. It's just that . . . I heard about it when the Deltas did that hospital visiting program."

"What? What!"

"Dace's sister."

"He doesn't have a sister," Vicki said. "He's the heir *and* the spare."

Alaina shook her head. "Denial. Classic denial. He has a sister. They were really really tight when they were kids. And then they discovered that she had a severe personality disorder. Within a matter of weeks, it turned into a full-blown psychosis."

"Say it in English. His sister went crazy?" said Vicki.

Alaina hesitated, then nodded. "Yes. They found out when she tried to kill Dace . . . tried to stab him to death. She's been . . . institutionalized ever since." She looked at Vicki. "I'm sorry. I shouldn't have told you . . ."

"No. No, I'm glad you . . ."

"You won't tell anyone will you? Promise."

"Promise," said Vicki mechanically, numb with shock.

"Not even Dace," said Alaina.

"No. Not even Dace."

"If you ever need to talk," offered Alaina.

Vicki shook her head.

Alaina waited for a minute, then said, "Well, I'm turning in early. 'Night, Vicki."

Vicki nodded. She knew it would be a long, long time before she fell asleep that night.

"Get the dancing shoes ready," he whispered.

The music began.

She laughed and started to dance. Then she couldn't stop laughing, couldn't stop dancing. Faster and faster the music played. Faster and faster she danced.

She tried to stop laughing to save her breath. But she couldn't.

She tried to stop dancing so she could breathe. But she couldn't.

Tears began to run down her face. "Please," she gasped. "Please, please."

Then the music stopped. She fell down. She reached for her shoes, tried to take them off. But they were too tight. They burned her hands.

Then a dark figure came toward her. Something glinted in its hand. An enormous knife.

The knife raised. And came flashing down.

Toward her ankles.

"Pleeeeeease," she screamed.

She was alone. Her room was dark, and empty. A quiet nightmare this time, one that didn't wake Alaina or Alan or her parents. One that only woke her.

I've got to tell someone, she thought.

I'll tell Janet.

Then, suddenly, she remembered something Janet had said, a long, long time ago. Something about her red shoes as art.

Janet.

No.

"I've got to talk to someone," she whispered. *Or I'll go crazy.*

And a little gibbering nasty voice deep inside answered, *Maybe you already have.*

"Are you and Dace doing it?"

"Doing what?" asked Vicki absently.

"Homecoming. The *dance*," said Janet with exaggerated patience.

"I don't know."

"Don't know? Don't *know*? Well, you don't know much, do you?" Then Janet stopped, and looked at Vicki more closely. Vicki turned her face away. What if Janet could read her thoughts — her madness — in her eyes?

"Vick? You okay?"

Get yourself to the reality zone, Vicki told herself. She forced herself to look at Janet, and to smile. "Well . . . it's nothing that a little homecoming invitation won't cure."

Janet's expression became cheerful again. "Don't you worry about that . . . uh-oh . . . maybe you should . . ."

"Vicki." Marty, wearing black leather pants and a black leather jacket and a black T-shirt, appeared like a dark angel beside them in the hall. His image reminded Vicki of something. Something . . . unpleasant. She drew back.

"Gotta go," said Janet, ignoring Vicki's mute look of appeal.

Marty didn't even acknowledge Janet's words. He planted his hands next to each side of Vicki's head, trapping her against the lockers.

"You've been treating me bad," he said softly.

"Marty, this is silly."

His face darkened. "Silly," he said.

"Well, no," she took it back hastily. "Not silly. But, we agreed . . ."

"I didn't agree to anything," said Marty. "I warned you . . ."

The dark figure with the knife, thought Vicki. The angel of death from her dream. Not Janet. No.

"Marty," she gasped.

He smiled and leaned closer. "Yes . . ."

"*Mister* Harmon. *Ms.* Clements."

Principal *Sewell*!

Marty looked into Vicki's eyes. "Later," he said. He pushed away from her and turned. "See ya," he said to the principal and sauntered away.

"Would that we all had what you apparently have to offer, Ms. Clements," said Principal Sewell. "I told you I'd be watching you, Clements. You've got problems, haven't you? You get in trouble *so* easily . . ." She was almost crooning now, leaning closer and closer.

Vicki leaned back helplessly.

"You're trouble, and I'm watching you. So anyone around you is going to get in trouble, too. Understand? Pass it along," she hissed.

She really is crazy, thought Vicki. And then she thought, what *does* she know about me?

For a long moment the principal studied her, as if Vicki were some puzzle. Then she nodded. "Get to class," she ordered brusquely.

Saved! Vicki headed in the opposite direction as fast as she could go, before Principal Sewell could change her mind.

Then she saw Caddie, lurking at the edge of the lockers, a vicious, triumphant expression on her face. And Vicki suddenly knew who to thank for her rescue from Marty. Trying to do Vicki dirty, Caddie'd actually helped out. Unexpectedly, Vicki felt better.

She raised her hand and gave a little wave. "Caddie. Thanks, babes. Stick around, and I'll show you how it's done. . . ."

She was still laughing at the shock on Caddie's face when she got to class.

Chapter 10

"Yes," said Vicki.

"Take your time," Dace teased. "Don't let me push you into anything."

She leaned against him. "Yes, yes, yes, yes, yes," she whispered.

Behind and above them, the bleachers were rocking. The Amelia Earhart Pilots were on a scoring drive.

"Well," said Dace. "I guess that means we're going to the homecoming dance." He kissed her beneath her ear. "Will you wear your red shoes for me?"

Vicki froze.

"Vicki?"

She pulled back.

"My red shoes?"

"Vicki, is something wrong?"

"Dace," she said. She stopped.

"Vicki," he answered. "What?"

"Dace, I . . . you don't think I'm crazy, do you?"

"Crazy?" He sat very still. "No. Wild and crazy, yes." The words were light, but his voice was dark.

Then Vicki remembered what Alaina had said. Dace's sister . . .

"Why?" Dace stared straight ahead, not looking at Vicki.

Vicki swallowed. "Well," she said. "I just told you I'd go to the homecoming dance, didn't I? I guess that does make me wild *and* crazy."

Dace shook his head.

Good going, Vicki, she told herself. Then, to her relief, he turned back toward her. "I guess it does," he said.

The night erupted in cheers. Touchdown, thought Vicki. Then Dace had pulled her to him and was kissing her hard, harder than he'd ever kissed her before.

"He asked me," Vicki told Janet the next morning.

"Fantastic. *F*antastic!"

"Yeah. I know what you mean. Now I just have to get my *daddy*'s permission."

They walked along in silence for awhile, scuffling up the leaves. Then Vicki said, "Well, if we double, no problem. Right?"

"Yeah. So has anyone asked you? You asked anyone?"

Janet shook her head. "No." She paused dramatically. "I'm just a reject in the homecoming invitation pile of life."

Vicki wasn't taken in. "Bored with everyone, huh?"

"Not *everyone*. Your brother, for instance . . ."

"Ask him."

"I couldn't do that," said Janet.

"Start subtle. Ask him up to see your etchings."

"Sculptings," corrected Janet. "I think."

"Art, then," said Vicki.

Janet looked at Vicki thoughtfully. "You know, Vicki, I don't just show what I'm working on to anybody. I mean, I'm serious about my art."

"No kidding."

"I mean it," said Janet, with sudden, uncharacteristic ferocity. She paused, then added, "Not that you've ever asked me to see it."

"Hey." Vicki was stung. "I'm trying to respect your privacy, but okay. Can I see what you're working on?"

A look of sudden panic crossed Janet's face. "No! I mean, no, not yet. I'm not ready . . ."

Vicki shook her head and after a moment Janet grinned like her normal self. They kept walking. Then Janet said, thoughtfully, "*Is* he going to the dance with anyone, do you know?"

"Alan! You scared me to death."

Her brother raised one eyebrow, then played a little tune on the horn of his car.

"The T-bird," said Vicki. "You haven't driven it since . . . in awhile."

"I figured it was time," said Alan. "Don't you think so?" He reached across and opened the door. "Want a ride?"

Vicki looked at the T-bird. It was just a car, she told herself. Her accident wasn't the car's fault. It wasn't anybody's fault. It was just an accident.

She raised her eyes slowly and met Alan's. They

had a funny expression in them. They looked —
sad?

Do it, she thought, and before she could let herself think about it anymore, she was sliding into the
car.

He slammed the door shut.

"Good woman," he said, and roared away from
the curb.

"It's good to be back in it," she said, and realized,
as the wind whipped past her, that she meant it.

"Where's Janet?"

"Cheerleading practice," she shouted cheerfully.

Alan grinned. "She got me!"

"What?"

"For the dance. Looks like we're going to be
doing the doubles."

"You asked her?"

Alan spun the wheel and they headed down the
ramp onto the interstate loop. "She asked me!"

Vicki laughed. She leaned back and laughed and
laughed as they flew around the loop. They were
going fast, faster, so fast that nothing, no one, could
catch her. And she was happy. The old exhilaration,
the almost manic joy, was burning through her
veins.

It was if the accident had never even happened.

And she didn't even have to ask her father about
the dance. Alan spiked it into the conversation,
slouched in the armchair in the den, watching an
old movie with Vicki and her Dad and Alaina. The
buckets of blood poured down on poor Sissy Spa-
cek's head and Alan said, "Yeah, that reminds me.

Janet and I are doubling up with Dace and Vicki for homecoming."

Rutland Clements had grinned. "That reminds you? I hope you do better than that for homecoming, Alan. At least get the girl a corsage."

Alan looked pained. "A corsage! But she asked me!"

"A corsage and *no jeans*," said Alaina sweetly.

Alan had howled. And that had been that.

"Ready?"

"Ready," said Vicki.

"Ready," said Lolly.

"Then let's do it — let's shop until we drop!" Janet led the way into the mall.

It was early Saturday morning and the Great Prom Dress Hunt was on.

Three hours later, they'd shopped. And Vicki was ready to drop.

"Golly gee whiz," said Janet sarcastically, slumping into a booth at the coffee shop. "Maybe you should have brought your dad along to help you find the perfect dress."

Vicki moaned. "I'm sorry. At least you have your dress, though."

"And it's just perfect for you, Janet," Lolly crooned. "Mine too. For me, I mean." Lolly patted the dress box next to her as if it were alive.

Janet relented a little. "We'll find something, don't worry."

"Easy for you to say," Vicki shot back.

"Well," said Janet, "we still have a couple of more stores. When the going gets tough, the tough go shopping." She slurped up the last of her Coke like a bad kid. "Let's get tough."

They found the dress, naturally, at the very last store.

"I can't believe it," said Vicki, turning back and forth in front of the mirror.

"Yeah," said Lolly. "I mean, like, I wouldn't even have gone into this store. It's like, for mothers and things, you know?"

Janet was grinning. "Not any mothers we know!"

Vicki's dress was just a tube, and a short tube at that. It fit. Very, very snugly. But over it was a jacket, a long, belted jacket with sleeves and a stand-up collar, a jacket that reached her knees, and flicked open just a little when she moved.

"Your father will never know," said Janet.

"Ooh," said Lolly. "You're going to wear the coat, aren't you? Just unbuttoned, right?"

"No!" Vicki shrugged the coat off and looked down. "What my father doesn't know won't hurt him. I just hope it stays up." She paused, then added thoughtfully. "Or maybe I don't."

Her eyes met Janet's in the mirror and then they both burst out laughing.

Lolly — whose own dress was a wedding cake of ruffles so artfully arranged that you didn't realize just what was missing until she turned and walked away and you saw her back — pouted. "I don't see what's so funny."

"Wh-why?" gasped Janet.

"Because. Because you could get into a lot of trouble with a dress like that."

That made them laugh even harder.

Chapter 11

It was folded up like a love note.

From Dace? wondered Vicki, pulling it out of her backpack. She read her name, printed in blue ballpoint pen, on the outside. When did he do this?

She unfolded the paper. Her eyes widened and her head jerked back as if she'd been punched.

No, she thought. I don't believe it.

But it was true. Whoever was after her had gotten her again. Her hand tightened convulsively on the paper, and then she was wadding it up, flinging it from her.

"No!" she hissed through clenched teeth. Holding her backpack at arm's length, as if it were a bomb, she turned and ran toward the back door of the school.

She would have kept on running, would have skipped school, and gone who knew where, except for Janet. Good old Janet.

Who was suddenly beside her. "Vicki? Vicki. Hey, slow down . . ."

Vicki slowed down. Stopped. Looked at Janet.

Her eyes filled with tears.

"You don't hate me, do you, Janet?"

"What are you talking about?"

"Someone hates me . . ." To Vicki's horror, the tears from her eyes spilled over and ran down her cheeks.

"Take it easy. No one hates you!"

"They do. They do!" Vicki gulped, forced herself to stop crying. "Someone left me a note. In my backpack. It said . . . it said . . ." She stopped, the tears threatening to overwhelm her.

"Let me see it," said Janet authoritatively.

"I threw it down. By my locker."

"Then we'll go find it. Come on."

Grateful for Janet's decisiveness, Vicki followed her back toward the junior locker section with uncharacteristic meekness.

"Now. Where did you throw it?"

"Right there. Over by the stairs. It was on white notebook paper. I wadded it up and threw it."

Janet walked in the direction Vicki was pointing. Bending over like a prospector, she inspected every inch of the floor around the lockers. At last she straightened up.

"No note," she said.

It's happening again, thought Vicki. This isn't real. She said aloud, slowly, clearly, as if Janet were a stubborn child, "I got a note. With horrible things written on it."

Janet wasn't Alan. She didn't lay the truth and belief line on Vicki. Instead she asked, "What did it say?"

Closing her eyes, Vicki recited, " 'Little Bo Peep/ has lost her shoes/and doesn't know where to find them/but leave them alone/and they'll come home/ dragging her feet behind them.' "

"That's it?" asked Janet. "That's the whole note?"

"What do you want? Blood? Guts? Death threats?" Vicki opened her eyes and glared at her best friend.

"Well," said Janet, "it's just a weirdo rhyme. It doesn't mean anything. I mean, I don't see why you're getting so upset."

"Don't you see? It's about . . ." Vicki stopped. She hadn't told Janet about the night of the red shoes. She hadn't told anyone.

Janet watched Vicki, puzzled.

"It just reminds me of those nightmares, that's all. And whoever it was who put those, those bugs, in my shoes in gym."

"It's not connected," said Janet. "You know, for all you know, like I said, that could have been meant for me."

"It wasn't," said Vicki vehemently. "I know it wasn't. I mean, nothing else has happened to you, has it?"

"No — but it hasn't to you either, has it?" said Janet reasonably.

And as far as Janet knew, nothing else *had* happened to Vicki. They were back where they started.

I could tell Janet everything now, thought Vicki. But if I do, would she believe me? Maybe I'm just being paranoid. Maybe it really is nothing.

But somewhere, deep inside, she knew it wasn't. Somewhere deep inside, that maniac voice gurgled, "Just because you're paranoid, doesn't mean someone isn't going to get you."

And it was the maniac voice she believed.

She was numb. Cold. From far, far away, she watched Ms. Green scratch math notes on the blackboard. From far, far away, she watched her own hand write the same notes down in her notebook.

Somewhere, the maniac voice gurgled on. Somewhere, another voice was saying, Stay this way. Cold. Still. Far, far away from everyone. Forget what people think. Then you'll be safe. Then no one can get you.

But someone could. Someone hated her. Hated her so much, so very much.

Who? And why?

What had she ever done but have a good time?

The bell rang.

And the answer registered in her head.

Marty. Marty with his Ring Around the Rosie and his brooding sex-crazed obsessions. Marty, who'd been fun, dangerously fun, always ready to go her one better, make the thrill a little wilder, a little more exciting. She'd broken up with him after the accident. Marty had been in the car with them when the accident happened: Marty and Alaina and Janet and Lolly.

Marty.

The cold was burned up by insane, scalding anger.

She was going to find Marty. And maybe kill him for this.

"Who the hell do you think you are?" She didn't wait for Marty to turn around. She didn't care that they were in the middle of the hall. She shoved him hard, across the oncoming stream of people, up against the wall.

"What the — Vicki!"

"Yes. Vicki. You had fun with Vicki, didn't you?"

His smile was maddening. She wanted to push it up his nose. "You bet."

The fury burned white hot inside her. "No one, no one treats me that way, you pig! You miserable excuse for a human being. You Rod Stewart joke."

That got to him. The smile left his face. He said flatly, "Just say what you've got to say."

"Someone's been trying to scare me. Or drive me crazy. And someone left me a note in my backpack . . . a nice, nasty nursery rhyme."

Marty just looked at her. By now, people had started giving them a wide berth. But they were rubbernecking just the same, like ghouls on the highway passing a bloody car wreck.

Socking his shoulder again, Vicki leaned toward Marty. "I've had it. And so have you. From now on, I'm watching you. I'm wise to you. You try anything else — you're dead. Dead meat!"

Marty began to shake his head slowly. "Babe," he said. "I don't know what you're talking about."

"Wrong answer," she snarled. "Dead wrong."

"Dead right." He lowered his voice. "People are enjoying this. I'm not. Let's go somewhere. We can talk."

"I'm through talking," said Vicki.

"I'm not," said Marty, and he clamped his hand on her shoulder in a vise-like grip, and steered her into the stairwell.

Now he shoved her against the wall.

"Tough guy," she sneered. "You want to talk. Talk."

"You're nuts, you know? The nursery rhyme stuff, whatever it is, it isn't me."

He stopped, considering, and then said, slowly, "But there is something I could tell you. It isn't me. But it has to do with you."

"Mystery man," said Vicki. "Except the only mystery is, how someone like you has lived so long."

He answered, slowly, with a little smile on his face as if he were enjoying himself now. "No. Not me. If I were you, I'd be the one worried about her life. You're safe with me, babes."

He opened the door to the stairwell. "Think about it. Think about me. Me and you. Then maybe we'll talk some more."

He paused. "You're right, you know. Someone out there doesn't love you. Tough life. Isn't it?"

"Go and die," she said, but he was already gone.

Dimly, she heard the slamming door echoed on the stairwell above her. Dimly, she heard the final bell ring.

The crazy spin of emotion had left her weak, and dizzy. She stayed against the wall. I wish, she thought. I wish I were dead.

Chapter 12

He's dead! *He's dead!*

Someone was screaming. Then people began to run — from the parking lot, where they were hanging out as usual before school started, waiting for the first bell; from the steps, where they could watch the scene before the doors opened; from everywhere, following the thin raw sound of the screaming.

Vicki didn't run. She'd been standing with Janet, just by the back door, when the awful screaming had started. She'd stayed there. "What is it?" she'd whispered hoarsely.

But somehow she knew. She just knew.

Janet, who hadn't run either, said, "I'll find out," and had raced down the steps to join the crowd.

It was quite a big crowd now, Vicki noted detachedly. Practically the whole school. A big, pushing, shoving mob.

If someone doesn't do something, her thoughts went on, it's going to get out of hand.

And then a short, sharp-edged figure strode past Vicki and out toward the elementary playground next door, neither hurrying nor dawdling. The outer fringes of the crowd grew quiet and still as the figure approached, and the silence spread in a ripple all the way through it.

The crowd parted. Principal Sewell marched through it, to a small clear space around the slides. Something dark lay on the ground there.

Vicki turned away and went inside to homeroom.

You had to hand it to her. Only Principal Sewell could have gotten the students back inside so quickly. Only Principal Sewell could have kept them under control while the wailing of ambulances and police cars sounded outside.

But even Principal Sewell couldn't stop the whispers, the rumors, the looks. And even Principal Sewell couldn't stop Caddie. Caddie, who'd found Marty. Caddie, her normally ruddy complexion pale, her blue eyes mad, who stepped in front of Vicki as she was leaving homeroom.

"You!" she hissed.

"Excuse me," said Vicki.

"You." Caddie's voice was rising, the hiss going up like the whistle of a kettle. "*Youuuu.*"

Heads turned. People stopped. Vicki was vaguely conscious of Lolly, just at the edge of her vision, her mouth dropping open.

Caddie didn't care. Or maybe she wanted everybody to stop and stare. Maybe she enjoyed it.

Vicki tried to edge around her, but Caddie blocked her way.

"*You killed Marty,*" she screamed. "*You did it. You did it!*"

By now the homeroom teacher had come out. She propelled Vicki to one side, and grabbed Caddie by the shoulders.

"*Murderer*," screamed Caddie.

"Stop it!" ordered the teacher. To Vicki she said, "Go. Go!"

And for the second time that day, Vicki watched a crowd grow quiet, and step aside. She walked between the rows of students, looking straight ahead, willing herself not to cry, not to faint.

And behind her Caddie's wailing dirge rose insanely. "*Murdererrrrrr!*"

By lunchtime, everyone knew.

Everyone knew that Marty had been found, bloody and crumpled, out by the sliding board at the elementary school.

Everyone knew that he wasn't dead — yet.

Everyone knew that he and Vicki had had a horrible fight just the day before.

Everyone knew what Caddie had said, before being taken home, still gesturing madly, still repeating her litany of hate and accusation.

Against Vicki.

"Forget it," Janet said at lunch. They were sitting in a corner, at Vicki's insistence. Somehow she felt safer with her back against the wall. That way, when she looked up, she could meet the accusing eyes of her classmates — instead of feeling them boring into her from behind.

"How can I forget it?" she said.

"Because no one *really* believes you had anything to do with it. They just like the spin. And Caddie.

People who know you and people who know Caddie — who're they going to believe?"

Janet waited.

Vicki shrugged.

Exasperated, Janet slammed her hand down on the table. "You. That's who. Nobody but you."

Vicki shrugged again.

"Listen. The only one who's watching you? Dace. 'Cause here he comes now."

It *was* Dace, walking through the tables, ignoring the heads turning, the stares. He was looking straight at Vicki, his expression unreadable. His sister, thought Vicki. He's remembering his sister. Does he think I'm like her? Crazy. Crazy enough for murder?

Something flickered in his eyes as he drew closer, and some part of Vicki shrank back, knowing it was true. Knowing that Dace, like Caddie, was about to condemn her, expose her in front of everyone.

"Vicki." He leaned over and before Vicki could do anything, gave her a kiss. A hard, dangerous kiss.

"Dace!" gasped Vicki, when he'd let her go.

"Public display of affection," mocked Janet. "I'd be careful if I were you."

"What are you doing here?" Vicki asked. "This isn't your lunch period."

"It is now," said Dace. He sat down astride a chair, his back to the room, and raised an eyebrow. "You save anything good for me?"

"Depends," said Vicki softly. I am going crazy, she thought, not to trust Dace. "Depends on what you had in mind." And for just a second she forgot to worry about the stares, the whispers.

He smiled.

"Go for vogue," said Janet softly. She stood up. "Now, if you don't mind, I'll just be going."

Everywhere she turned for the rest of the day, Dace was there, but a Dace she'd never seen: more aggressive, more remote, more in control somehow. And protective.

And when he met her at the locker after school, Janet was there. And Lolly. And Alaina. They formed a little group around Vicki and walked with her out of the school.

Lolly kept glancing at Vicki, her eyes shining with curiosity. But then, that was Lolly. At least she was there.

When they reached the street, the roar of Alan's T-bird drowned out all the other sounds — even the little murmurs of conversation Vicki could imagine she was hearing.

He pulled to a stop at the foot of the front steps.

"Get in," he said.

And they did, all except Dace. "I'll talk to you later," he said softly, his lips brushing her ear.

They got in the car. Alan shifted into first. And Vicki felt her courage returning. Some impulse sparked her to turn around. To face the little knots of people standing and watching.

She waved. She waved at all of them.

"I'll see you," she shouted. "I'll see you tomorrow."

When she turned around, Alan, driving with white-knuckled ferocity, called back, *"Yeah."*

And Vicki knew she would be all right.

I *can* take it, she thought. I can take anything. I won't be beat.

It wasn't until much, much later that she realized that everyone in the car had also been there the night of her accident.

Everyone except Marty.

Chapter 13

People do forget.

Well, it wasn't as simple as that, thought Vicki, leaning back in the bathtub. They hadn't forgotten. They'd just gotten distracted by other things, so that one day not everyone looked over their shoulders when she walked into a room. And then another day. And then another.

Not that her life was back to normal. But every day Janet and Alaina and even Lolly and Alan had been there for her, showing people that they believed in Vicki, steamrolling the rumors with their scorn for it all, keeping even a momentarily subdued, but still sullen and resentful Caddie, at bay.

And Dace. She lingered over the thought of him. He'd been solid. When everyone was down, he'd stood up. For her.

Even Marty's being in a coma could only be hot gossip for so long. It was like those sleazy newspapers, Vicki's mind ran on. Headline today, last page tomorrow, kitty litter liner the last.

Although I don't exactly like to think of myself as kitty litter liner material, she thought wryly.

She sighed and slid deeper into the bubbles. Their heady scent filled the steamy bathroom. She felt weightless, free.

"Vicki!" Pounding on the door, then Alaina's head around the corner of it. Vicki shrieked and crossed her hands across her chest, sliding lower into the water.

"It's just me, silly," said Alaina. "Are you going to be in here all night? Alan just beat me to the bathroom upstairs, and I'd like to get ready for the dance, too."

"No, *really*?" said Vicki sarcastically.

"Vicki!" wailed her normally calm sister.

"All right, all right," said Vicki. Alaina was entitled to be a little nervous. She was the Deltas' choice for homecoming queen. Of course, it didn't hurt her chances that she had just started dating Thom Nixx, everyone's choice for most beautiful, most handsome, most likely to succeed guy in school.

Except Dace, Vicki told herself. Compared to Dace, Thom Nixx is just another pretty face.

She stood up and reached for her towel.

"Like a firing squad," muttered Alan, baring his teeth.

"Hold it, hold it!" ordered their father. The three Clements stood lined up in front of the fireplace: Alaina, regal in an ice-blue dress that somehow showed her off without showing anything; Alan, in the middle, dressed up as only Alan could be dressed up for a formal dance and get away with it; and Vicki on the other side, her coatdress buttoned up to the neck.

Their father fired away. Pop, pop, pop, until Vicki was seeing stars.

"Now, each couple alone," he commanded.

As Alan groaned audibly, Alaina said, "Thom and I'll go first, since we need to get there early."

"Who'd ever guess your father was a flash freak," whispered Janet to Alan.

Silently, Vicki reached over to pull Dace into place for their couple shot. It was a pain, but so what? It kept her father placated. She was going to the dance with Dace, and that was all that counted.

"Smile," ordered her father. But Vicki didn't need to be told. Tonight, it was easy to smile.

The gym shone like a carnival funhouse in the night. The parking lot was already crowded, and Alan, ever protective of his Bird, drove it to the back corner of the lot.

"You could have dropped us off first," teased Janet.

"It's a long, lonely walk," Alan told her. He added, as they threaded their way through the parking lot, caught in the strobe lights of more cars pulling in, "Hey, think of this parking lot as the unfriendly skies . . . and these guys, the ones who don't just say no? Think of how they'll be flying low soon — no way I'm leaving my car in their flight path, y'know?"

Vicki slid one hand into Dace's. With the other, she began working on the top button of her coat.

"Need some help?" Dace's other hand closed over hers. She stopped and turned to face him, and stood obediently still as he unbuttoned the rest of the buttons.

"I like what I see," he said.

"You haven't seen anything yet," said Vicki. "Wait till we get inside the gym."

Inside, it was the same old corny autumn theme, mixed with the school colors. Since the school colors were red and white, the contrast with the autumn branches and pots of mums and other fall touches didn't quite work. But in the dim light and the rush of music, it somehow didn't matter.

Vicki thought, I have never seen anything so romantic in my life. And laughed at herself.

"May I take your jacket?" asked Dace.

Alan had grabbed Janet's hand to pull her out onto the dance floor, but she stopped him and turned expectantly.

Vicki stood for a moment, savoring the attention. Then she reached up and in one motion stripped the jacket away.

"Yeah!" said Janet. "Let's dance. Alan?"

But Alan was standing, staring at Vicki. "Well, well, little sister," he said.

"Weird brother," said Dace softly.

"Weird sister, maybe," said Janet suddenly, her eyes narrow, as if she were looking at Vicki from Alan's point of view. "Alan, come on!" She yanked Alan away.

Vicki turned around to give Dace the full effect, then held out her foot. "And the red shoes? See?"

"And like," he said.

"Just your basic dress," she said slyly, allowing him to lead her out onto the floor to dance.

* * *

The night passed like a dream.

"May I cut in?" Alan. Dace danced easily over to Janet. Alan cleared his throat, then said, "Has Alaina seen you?"

"Oh, Alaina. Don't worry. She's worried about homecoming queen. She doesn't care what I wear."

She pulled back a little. Alan was holding her so tightly!

"Alan?"

"Well, maybe you'll get her some extra votes, at that."

Vicki stopped dancing. "What do you mean?"

"No one else is dressed like you, that's all."

Vicki picked up the beat. "That's the point, Alan dear."

"Is it, sister dear?"

"Believe it," she told him.

Principal Sewell was standing near one of the tables, watching them. Take that, thought Vicki, giving a little shimmy. Bet you wish you could do this. She gave Dace a quick kiss as she danced by.

I could dance all night.

Other dances, other guys. Some of them danced on her feet. Some of them pushed their luck. Some of them were drunk and unfunny. Some of them were fun, fun, fun.

And she always danced back to Dace.

And then the lights went even lower, the drummer launched an elaborate roll, and the spotlights went up on the stage erected at the far end of the gym.

Vicki kept dancing, a little dance in place, as the homecoming drill proceeded. She danced for each member of the court.

And she danced for the long, long time it took, as bad as any Academy Awards night, for Principal Sewell — for it was indeed she, in a dress that was somehow just a longer, somewhat shinier version of one of her suits — to unfold the little piece of paper, silently read the words written there, clear her throat, and announce in a flat, unemotional voice, the new homecoming queen.

Alaina.

Vicki spun around and threw her arms around Dace. "She did it," she cried. "She did it."

And danced a victory dance right there for her sister.

As the dancing started again, led by the shining new queen, Dace caught Vicki's arm.

"Let's catch some time out," he said.

So Vicki danced alongside Dace, back through the crowd, back, quickly out a side door so the chaperones couldn't see them, and out to the parking lot and the T-bird.

"It's not so lonely out here after all," said Vicki, seeing how close other cars were parked to Alan's, in spite of all his precautions. She patted the nose of the T-bird.

"I'm lonely," said Dace, who'd slipped up onto the hood. "C'mere."

"Maybe," said Vicki, spinning around for the sheer joy of it.

"C'mon," said Dace. "Fly a little lower. Or better yet, put down some landing gear."

Still spinning, Vicki tilted back her head and laughed. Laughed at herself. Laughed at the spinning stars above. Laughed at how strong and good she felt.

"Coming," she said. "Coming in for a landing."

And she fell, still laughing, into Dace's arms.

Chapter 14

"Mmmm." She shifted languorously. "Mmmm."

"Warm enough?" murmured Dace.

"Mmmm . . . yes. And no."

Somehow, they'd gotten inside the T-bird. Less space than the hood, but warmer and more private.

Dace pulled back. "Listen. I'm going to go get the rest of your dress . . ." Vicki could sense, rather than see, that he was smiling. "And my jacket. Meanwhile, take this coat."

Dreamily, she allowed him to pull his suit coat over her shoulders. She leaned back into it, and watched him slide out of the car.

"Dace," she said.

"Yeah?"

"Hurry," she said.

She saw the glint of his grin this time, before he hurried into the darkness.

She pulled the coat around her shoulders, feeling Dace's warmth still in it. The gym, the dance, the whole world seemed far, far away. She closed her eyes after awhile, and let her thoughts drift. Pleasantly.

"Vicki."

Such a soft sound. She opened her eyes. "Dace?"

"Vicki . . . Vicki."

Vicki sat up and looked back across the parking lot. A few dark figures weaving in and out among the cars. The gym, with the faint sound of music coming from it.

"Vickiii."

Almost a whisper. Vicki turned her head, then opened the car door.

"Vicki."

Someone was calling her. And it sounded like . . . it sounded like . . . Vicki tilted her head, listening intently.

"Vicki." Hardly more than a breath this time, but Vicki had pinpointed the source.

The playground.

No way, she thought. I'm not gonna fall for that.

"Vicki."

She shivered. Where was Dace? She strained to see if he might be coming back, but saw no one.

"Vicki."

"No," she said aloud, softly. And waited.

The voice stopped.

The music from the gym seemed to grow louder.

This is bull, she thought, the old anger suddenly welling up in her. I'm not going to let this happen.

I'm not going to take it anymore.

She slammed the car door behind her. The sound was like a shot. She jumped, and her heart started racing, really racing, the adrenaline started burning through her veins.

"I'm coming," she said aloud. "And you'd better watch out."

She stalked forward, heedless of the uneven ground, until she got to the edge of the playground.

"Who's there?" she demanded.

A sharp edge of wind cut through the dark, keening slightly. Nothing else made a sound.

"Who is it! Who are you?"

Something moved.

Vicki jumped. She twisted around.

Creak creak creak. One of the swings, caught by the wind.

Then, on the other side of the playground, a noise as loud as a pistol shot.

Fear froze the anger in her veins for a moment, and then she realized it was just a seesaw.

She gave a little snort of disgust. She faced the sound. "I'm not afraid," she said. "I'm not afraid of you anymore."

And the hands closed around her throat.

She was drowning. Drowning. The pounding of the water, the rush of death.

It was her own head, her own blood, the violent jumping of her heart as she fought to breathe.

The awful grip on her throat was gone. She tried to breathe. It hurt.

Dimly, she became aware of cold metal beneath her hands, cold metal beneath her knees. The keening wind burned ice into her bare skin. Dace's jacket was gone.

The hands were still there. Looser, but still there. She raised her head slightly, and they tightened, just a little, just enough to let her know.

She was on the sliding board, on her hands and knees, facing out over the playground. Somehow, she'd been dragged up onto the sliding board.

The hands tightened a little more.

"Don't struggle," a hoarse whisper warned. "You see how easy it is." The hands tightened again and Vicki coughed, straining to breathe.

"Understand?"

"Huuuh." She nodded weakly.

"Good. Stand up."

Vicki tried. But her legs were shaking so hard, she couldn't.

She was jerked violently backward. The pressure of the hands stopped the scream in the throat.

"Stand up!"

This time, awkwardly, her head and neck held in the noose of fingers, she succeeded.

Her tormentor stood up behind her. Soft, excited breath brushed past her ear. It was repellent, and it was that, not the wind, that made her shiver this time.

She looked out over the playground. There was the gym, full of normal people doing normal things: dancing, laughing, talking, flirting. Happy people. Tears filled her eyes.

I'm going to die, she thought.

She tried to turn.

"Stand still."

And so she stood still, in her red shoes, on top of the sliding board, no different from a diving board, really, if she thought about it, death was just a dive away. . . .

The voice began to chant.

Vicki's panicked, reeling thoughts stopped.

"This little sister went to market. This little sister stayed hoooome. This little sister had roast beeef. This little sister had nooone. . . . And this little sister cried . . . are you crying, little sister? This little sister cried . . ."

And it all came back.

She was standing in the back of the car, her arms outspread. She could see Alan's golden hair flying below her as he drove, Janet and Lolly squeezed in the front seat, looking back up at her, Alaina in the back on one side of her, holding on to her legs to steady her, Marty on the other.

And then. And then — someone had pushed her.

Out. Up. Soaring. Too quick to be scared, just giddy disbelief and the slow, agonizing fall to darkness.

Someone had let go of her legs and pushed her.

"Alaina?" said Vicki.

The wind blew. Far away the dancing music played.

". . . Alaina.

"It is you, isn't it? You pushed me out of the car. And you were there that night, after my date with Dace. You laughed at me."

Vicki tried to turn, but the hands tightened warningly.

Trying to keep her voice calm, Vicki went on. "And it was you who did that to my shoes after gym. And left those shoes for me to find. Those bloody shoes."

A soft laugh. "Papier mâché. Thank Janet."

"The note in my backpack was you, too."

"Yess."

The wind plucked at both of them. It plucked at Vicki's heart.

"No wonder I had bad dreams," said Vicki, almost to herself.

Alaina began to laugh. "*I* gave you the bad dreams. It was so easy. All I had to do was come into your room after you were asleep, and hold my hand over your mouth. That's all."

Nausea rose in Vicki's throat. "Why?"

"I love you," the voice crooned. "I've always loved you. When you were little you needed me. Daddy was so proud of what good care I took of you."

The voice changed. "But you shouldn't have been born. *I* was the only girl. Daddy loved me best. And then you were born. No matter how much trouble I got you in, no matter how clumsy you seemed, he only loved you more . . . and you didn't need me anymore. That little pest Janet. Your best friend . . . And then Dace. . . .

". . . I hate you. . . ."

Alaina's grip tightened.

Vicki gagged, choked. "A-Alaina! What about Marty? Was that you, too?"

"Marty? He knew. He knew I pushed you. I heard him on the stairwell. He had to die."

"Alaina. He's not dead. You can still — "

"No! You . . . Daddy . . . I'm tired . . . so tired."

Now the hands tightened again.

"Alaina! Please!" Vicki reached up and desperately tried to pry the iron fingers from her neck. The darkness roared in her ears.

The car roared out of nowhere, the bright lights flashing on, pinning them in the headlight beams, pinning them to the sky.

Vicki jerked forward, trying to pull free. She caught one of Alaina's hands, and held tight.

The screaming tore the night. And she was flying, holding onto her sister's hand, flying into the dark.

And falling.

Chapter 15

"Good old Amelia Earhart," said Vicki, stopping at the foot of the stairs. The day was cold and brilliantly clear, and the red brick building looked warm and friendly in the sparkling sunlight.

"Keep your voice down," said Janet. "Or people will think it was your head and not just your collarbone that was broken."

The clusters of people on the stairs were drifting slowly inside, a concession to the cold. Some of the students looked over at Vicki and Janet. A few whispered.

But Vicki didn't mind. What people say is never going to bother me again, she thought. It's what I know that is important. She shrugged her backpack carefully a little higher on her right shoulder. Her left shoulder and arm were immobilized in a sling until her broken collarbone healed. This sling is the worst, thought Vicki. Talk about fashion victims!

"So how is Alaina?" Janet asked.

Good old Janet, thought Vicki. She never meets anything less than head on.